D1153057

Phantom Horse
Goes to Scotland

Books in the series

PHANTOM HORSE
PHANTOM HORSE COMES HOME
PHANTOM HORSE GOES TO IRELAND
PHANTOM HORSE IN DANGER
PHANTOM HORSE GOES TO SCOTLAND
WAIT FOR ME PHANTOM HORSE

Phantom Horse
Goes to Scotland

CHRISTINE PULLEIN-THOMPSON

illustrated by
Eric Rowe

AWARD PUBLICATIONS LIMITED

ISBN 0-86163-848-4

Text copyright © Christine Pullein-Thompson 1981
Illustrations copyright © Award Publications Limited 1997

This edition first published 1997 by
Award Publications Limited,
27 Longford Street, London NW1 3DZ

Printed in Italy

1

It was summer. We were sitting in the garden with the hum of the bumble-bees in our ears and the apple-blossom like snow upon the grass.

"Must you go? Can't you say no for once?" I asked.

Dad shook his head. "I wish I could, but it's a matter of life and death," he said.

"It always is," said Angus with bitterness in his voice.

"We'll miss all the shows, and Phantom is just ready. He's at his peak. You realise that, don't you?" I asked.

"Stop it, do you hear? Stop it!" cried Mum. "It's your father's duty to go, and my duty to go with him."

"I know what we can do," said Angus. "I've thought it all out. There's this most marvellous place in Scotland where you can be coached. Couldn't you send us there?"

"Coached? Coached in what?" asked Dad, sitting up straight on his sun-lounger.

"In almost anything actually," replied Angus, suddenly sounding confident.

"In maths? Can you be coached in maths?" asked Mum.

"Yes, and in pottery, and sailing, and you can be taught high-class riding, the sort Jean likes – dressage, instructors' certificates, the lot. It's in the Sunday paper. Hang on, I'll get it," finished Angus, disappearing at high speed.

Phantom grazed in the orchard, gold and silver, beautiful beyond words. I saw myself learning dressage, returning, riding in horse trials. I imagined Scotland – purple hills, grey houses, men in kilts, bagpipes playing.

"Here's the article about it – look, I've marked it," said Angus, handing Dad a Sunday paper. "The school is called The Island School and College of Further Education. The headmaster is a Mr Carli."

"What a romantic name for a school," said Mum.

We watched Dad reading the newspaper report. There were dark circles under his eyes. I suddenly realised that he did not want to leave home once again, that Mum was right. He was only going because his conscience told him to. Sparrow Cottage dreamed behind us in the summer sun. We all loved it, but if you are in the Foreign Office you go where you are sent.

"It seems all right on the surface. What do

you think, darling?" he asked, handing Mum the paper.

Over her shoulder, I read an article about a school on an island called Uaine where you could ride, swim and snorkel, where you could be coached in maths, French and Latin, where seals played on white sand and sheep grazed the hills. It sounded fantastic.

"It will be very expensive," Mum said. "So you must make full use of the amenities."

"We'll have to get some references. You can't just go off into the blue for five weeks," Dad said.

But they were pleased. "It's a solution anyway. A bearable one, and much better than having Aunt Nina again," muttered Angus.

"And not too far for Phantom," I added.

"I suppose you have to take him?" asked Dad.

"Yes, he'll be turned into a dressage horse and come back worth thousands," I answered. "Besides, I always take him."

"And Killarney will go to Dominic, because Scotland isn't his sort of country," said Angus.

I thought of Dominic, who loves grey Killarney, riding him through the tall beech-woods; Dominic who is our best friend, sometimes our only friend, and I felt very happy.

"I can't wait to go," I decided. "I've never lived on an island before. Will there be cars?"

"We'll find out. I'll write straight away," replied Dad, leaping to his feet. "I envy you; it's going to be much more fun than the Middle East."

I think I should explain that Dad is a sort of diplomatic troubleshooter. He assesses difficult situations abroad and reports back to the government. Mum goes with him because they are also expected to socialise, and because she thinks Dad needs her.

We went to the local comprehensive school, and Angus had failed his maths after a retake in the autumn. If extra coaching at The Island School could get him through the exam, our parents wouldn't hesitate to send him.

A week later a letter came back with photographs of a grey house with turrets at each end; and of prefabricated classrooms. There was a list of courses you could follow – pottery and needlework, riding and swimming, as well as more academic subjects. There were letters from satisfied clients and photographs of Highland ponies; teachers, including the headmaster, lined up by a stately front door; and a dormitory with duvets on the beds.

Dad said, "It's qualifications which count and there seem plenty here," in satisfied tones.

"What about a bit of domestic science, Jean?" suggested Mum.

I shook my head. "I just want to ride," I said, "to become really good at dressage and pass my A Test with the Pony Club."

"We'll put you down for domestic science anyway," Mum said. "It will be for life."

"Not for me, please. When I have my riding-school I won't have time for anything but horses," I replied.

Later I tacked up Phantom and rode to the

farm where our friend Dominic lived.

When I had finished telling him about Uaine, he said, "So you're off again, Jean. You'll miss the local horse show. Don't you mind about that?"

"Yes, but this is going to be the experience of a lifetime, and there are more important things than shows," I answered, quoting Mum.

"You could have stayed with us," he said.

"I'll write. I'll send you gorgeous postcards."

"You'll miss Milestone and his rider; they're coming to demonstrate to the Pony Club," continued Dominic. "You know, he's the greatest Australian showjumper of all time. The team is in Britain for the summer, competing in all the big shows and getting ready for the next Olympics."

"One always misses something if one goes away; it's inevitable," I said.

"Well, you know I'm here if you need me. You've got the number," said Dominic.

"I know it by heart," I replied.

"How's Phantom travelling then?"

"Dad's fixing him up. He's got this marvellous secretary who can fix anything."

Dominic looked at me with his grey-blue eyes. "Be careful," he said. "Scots can be awkward at times."

"Mum's Scottish and she's never awkward," I said. "Angus will be bringing Killarney over tomorrow. You do want him, don't you? You can ride him at the show. He's entered and he's sure to be placed in the hunter class."

I was disappointed with Dominic. I had wanted him to share my excitement, to be envious. But he never went anywhere because it was always milking time, or harvest time, or time for drilling; so he knew nothing about discovering new places.

"I'll write," I said, turning Phantom round. "Don't work too hard."

"I'll keep an eye on the cottage. Have a good time."

Dominic stood waving as I rode away, fair-haired, tall and immensely strong. I wish he would travel, I thought, then he would have something to talk about besides the sugar beet and the calving. He's becoming staid and dull, and he's only eighteen.

Soon we were packing. We were going by train to a town called Teanga and then across the sea to Uaine. Phantom was going to Perth with two brood mares and then on by private plane. Incredibly, the school had its own plane which could be used to carry horses. Mr Carli, the headmaster, had arranged his journey while on the phone to Dad.

"They won't load him," I said over and over again. "They'll never get him beyond Perth."

But no one would listen to me.

Dad was so busy doing "paperwork" on the Middle East that we hardly saw him, and Mum was occupied taking valuables to the bank, and buying clothes suitable for a hot climate.

Angus and I packed nearly all our clothes – I had warm jerseys, summer clothes, my riding-hat, two pairs of jodhpurs, three pairs of jeans, my one and only summer dress, a swimsuit and a bikini, plus shoes, pants, riding-boots and a host of other things. When I had finished my case weighed a ton. Then I started packing for Phantom.

Angus rode Killarney down to the farm while I groomed Phantom because I wanted him to arrive bright and shining, like gold. All the time I was imagining the island with seals sunning themselves on rocks, and the cry of gulls. Phantom was fidgety, as though he knew we were soon to be moving on, and every few minutes he neighed for Killarney.

"You're going on a plane," I told him. "Be sensible, keep calm. It's going to be all right." But he only stared into the distance and neighed.

Next day he followed me up the ramp into a horse box, calm and trusting. I hated leaving him. It was like a betrayal.

"Don't worry," said the driver, "we'll take good care of him."

"He won't go on the plane," I said, my eyes suddenly full of ridiculous tears. "I know he won't . . ."

"He will. I've never failed to load a horse yet," replied the driver, climbing into the cab, reversing, and driving away into a bright summer morning and to Scotland.

"You're not crying, are you?" asked Angus, staring at me suspiciously.

"No, I'm not," I shouted. "Why should I cry?"

I rushed indoors, imagining Phantom fighting on a runway, until in desperation he fell over backwards and broke his neck. I imagined a message arriving, saying simply: *Horse dead. Letter following.* I wished I had gone with him.

"All right? Has he gone?" asked Mum, combing her hair in front of the hall mirror.

"Yes."

"You're not crying, are you?" she asked, turning round. "Oh, Jean, you are a goose. He'll be all right."

"He won't get on the plane. I know he won't," I cried.

"He'll be all right. I know he will," she said.

"I should have gone with him."

"You know you couldn't. There wasn't room," said Mum, putting an arm round me. "Cheer up. You'll be there yourself in two days."

Next morning the telephone rang.

I stood shouting, "Telephone!" then answered it myself, certain that it was from Perth airport telling me that Phantom had slipped on the runway and was dead.

"It's Mr Carli," a voice said, "the headmaster of The Island School. I rang to say your horse has arrived and is in good shape." His voice was soothing; the kind doctors use when they are explaining something to a patient.

"Thank you, Mr Carli, thank you very much," I answered.

"Is that Jean?"

"Yes."

"We look forward to having you. Have a good journey," said Mr Carli.

I put down the receiver and rushed into the garden, shouting, "Phantom's arrived. He's all right. The headmaster rang. He sounds nice, very nice. He must have known how I felt. He must be nice to ring like that. He must be fond of horses . . ."

"Must you be so exaggerated, Jean? Phantom is only a horse," Dad said wearily, looking up from a pile of papers.

"But he's arrived. He's there waiting for me. I'm going to get everything ready in the hall. What time do we leave tomorrow?"

"Not until six in the evening. You're booked into a sleeper on the train," said Dad with a sigh, returning to his papers.

We checked everything. Counted our money for the tenth time – we each had plenty, because there might be no bank on the island. I put a book called *Dressage From Novice to Prix St George* by H. Goodfellow in my hand luggage, and Angus packed old maths papers.

We went to bed and I dreamed I was in a cave with no way out, and Phantom was drowning in dark, oily waters. I was thankful when morning came at last, pale pink and grey. The orchard looked empty without our horses, while far away the roar of commuter traffic was already beginning.

The day dragged. Mum and Dad packed, we locked the windows and put out the oil-fired Aga in the kitchen.

"We will simply drop you," Dad said. "Go straight to platform five; we will be going on to the airport."

"Mr Carli will meet you at Teanga," Mum told us. "Don't talk to strangers."

Then at last it was time to go. We took sandwiches with us and a Thermos of coffee. Our parents' suitcases were labelled and Mum wore a strange hat and a new blue suit. The station was crowded when we reached it.

"I'm parked on a double yellow line. Go," shouted Dad, as we fumbled with our luggage and kissed Mum goodbye.

Our train was in. Angus started to sing. I thought of Phantom waiting for me somewhere on an island as I turned to wave a final good-bye to Mum and Dad.

"Hurry, let's find where we are," shouted Angus, running along the train. "This is going to be the best holiday ever, except for the maths."

"It will be like going home," I answered. "I wish our Scottish granny was still alive . . ."

"We're free," said Angus, leaning out of a window. "For a whole month we can do what we like, except for maths. I've packed Grandpa's binoculars, the ones he had in the war. I'm going to bird-watch."

I wondered if it was true, if we were really free, and, as the train left the station, whether it was ever possible to be really free.

"Stop thinking about Phantom, look at the scenery," cried Angus. "Wasn't it clever of me to find the place? Aren't you grateful?"

"Yes. But we aren't there yet," I said.

"The mountains and the sea will meet; there will be salmon and lobster for dinner, and handsome young men who will flatter you," Angus said. "It will be a holiday to remember."

2

As we drew near the end of our journey, the train stopped more often, picking up ladies with shopping bags, children with buckets and spades, men with fishing-tackle. Then we could glimpse the sea. There were wild, beautiful hills and the cry of gulls, and low crofts perched among the hills like birds nesting. Then we could see tall masts and almost smell the sea. We stood at the corridor window, staring out on a wide bay.

"We had better get our things," said Angus, his voice trembling with excitement. "We're almost there."

The ticket-collector walked down the platform calling, "Teanga. All change!" Children ran down the corridor, their voices high-pitched with excitement. A woman pushed past us with two terriers on a lead. Doors were being flung open, we seized our cases, while outside voices called, "Hello. Did you have a good journey?" Then a child's voice cried, "Granny!"

We threw our cases out. The air was soft on our faces.

"That must be him. Look, over there. He's looking at us," cried Angus.

Mr Carli was tall, with dark hair which was silver at the temples. He had a scar which ran down one cheek like the cut of a knife. He held out a hand. "It's nice to meet you," he said. "Did you have a good journey?"

We nodded, suddenly tongue-tied. His handshake nearly left my hand in pieces. His face was deeply lined, but there was an air of energy

about him which made his age impossible to guess. He wore a gold cross inside his summer shirt, cotton trousers and sandals.

"Phantom is grand, Jean," he said, taking my case. "He's settled in just fine."

There were cars waiting for a ferry. The houses on the edge of Teanga met the hills and were lost amid the heather. The sun shone on our backs.

"This way," said Mr Carli, "I'm taking you. I have my own boat. That's Uaine." He pointed across a shimmering sea to an island shaped like a Cornish pasty, but green and purple instead of pastry-coloured, with hills, bays and trees, and the white spray of the sea breaking against her rocks. "Jump in. We'll be there in twenty minutes," said Mr Carli.

"What a wonderful place!" exclaimed Angus. "How did you find it? You're not Scottish, are you?"

Mr Carli shook his head. "I wanted to escape, to leave behind the noise and the bustle. Uaine is my newest venture. I'm still developing it. Next year there will be chalets, a heated swimming-pool, and a covered riding-school, Jean." He turned to smile at me and his eyes were the strangest I had ever seen, very dark with large pupils. They seemed to be somewhere else even while they looked at you.

"I ride myself," he continued, "and I want to

develop my own breed of horse – a Uaine Island horse, a cross between a Highland and a Donsky; and for your information, Donskies are Russian and the colour of Phantom."

I don't know how you would describe Mr Carli's boat. I am not an expert in such matters. It looked half ferry, half speedboat. It had a closed-in cabin, wooden seats and life-jackets, and smelled of tobacco. Mr Carli took the wheel. He wore a bracelet and his brown hands were covered with fine, dark hairs.

"What does Uaine mean?" asked Angus, after a short silence.

"It's Gaelic for green. My island may not look very green to you, but it's a lot greener than the others in this part of the world, and extremely fertile," said Mr Carli.

"It must be lovely to own an island: it must make you feel like a king," mused my brother.

We were nearly there. Every second things grew larger. Dark dots from a distance became rocks, ribbons of white became water falling down crevices in the hills. There was yellow gorse, bright pink flowers amid the rocks, seaweed, fine white sand, and birds everywhere.

"It's paradise," said Angus.

A man in a cap moored our boat. "This is Jacques. He hails from Brittany. He's here for the summer," explained Mr Carli.

I held out a hand, but Jacques ignored it. He

had resentful eyes under his peaked cap, half
hidden by a mop of dark hair.

"He's a funny chap. He'll take your cases to
the house. Come up to the square. Let me show
you the way," offered Mr Carli.

"The square?" I asked.

"The stables, the old ones. The new ones are
yet to be built," replied Mr Carli.

I could hear children laughing and someone
blowing a whistle. The air was soft and damp,
and there wasn't a cloud in the sky.

"We were very busy," said Mr Carli. "But we
broke up officially last week, and now there are
only the odd-bods left. Two of the teachers have
gone home until the autumn, and the indoor
staff are a bit depleted too. But you will be all
right. Angus will pass his maths exam, I
promise."

"At last," said Angus. "What a relief that
will be."

The square was simply of buildings with a
wall in front and iron gates – a sort of fenced-
in yard.

"I will leave you now, Jean," said Mr Carli.
"Caroline will look after you. She is my daughter and fully qualified. She will teach you
everything you need to know about horses."

Phantom whinnied when I called to him. He
was in an old-fashioned loose box with iron
bars topping wooden partitions, an iron hay-

rack and deep wooden manger. It was bedded with peat. He put his muzzle against the bars and nickered. "Are you all right? Did you miss me?" I said, then a voice asked:

"Does he look all right? I'm Caroline, your instructor. Pleased to meet you." She wore a checked shirt, jodhpurs, and long riding-boots. Her ginger hair was flecked with grey, her eyes a hard, clear grey. She looked what Dad would call 'a hard cookie'. She looked old for her age where her father looked young for his. Her mouth turned down at the corners and her teeth were stained. Only her nose resembled Mr Carli's.

"I thought you would be Scottish," I exclaimed, shaking her work-worn hand.

"You know the difference, then," her laugh sounded like the rasping of a hoof. It wasn't real. "They are all seeking their fortunes elsewhere," she said, and then added, "I'm looking forward to teaching you. It has been nothing but beginners for months now, and I'm not really that sort of teacher. I'm better at dressage and the finer points of riding. Any fool can keep saying, 'Toes up, don't lean forward, look straight ahead,' that sort of thing. I like the advanced stuff."

"Fantastic," I exclaimed. "I've passed my C and B tests; but the B was touch and go, and I only scraped through."

"I can see we are going to get on," said Caroline. "Do you want to see the other horses? We are building up a herd and there are a couple of ponies for the little kids, but that's about all." She whistled as she walked – tunelessly. I wished Angus was with me as we walked in silence along a path to a field where daisies grew amid the grass. The Highland ponies whinnied when they saw us. They were strange colours –

blue roans, orange and blue duns, the sort of colours which melted into the landscape. They had large kind eyes, marvellous feet and their own special smell. There was Flora, Ivan, Heather, Shadow and an old grey mare called Lassie.

"Next year the mares will be put in foal to a Donsky stallion," said Caroline. The two other ponies were half Shetland, black, and called Sinbad and Sailor. They felt our pockets hopefully and then, finding we had no titbits, swung their heels towards us in disgust.

"Nasty little things," said Caroline, "and completely spoilt. You start your lessons tomorrow at ten. If you ever want me, I'm in the third cottage on the left, the one with the crooked chimney. If you follow the path through the rhododendrons you will reach the front of the house. All right?"

I nodded. Feeling very far from home, I waved and then ran, and a warm breeze straight from the sea blew against my face. I followed the path and came out on a lawn and there was the house, grey and severe with turrets at each end, and beyond it the prefabricated buildings with concrete paths between. I slowed to a walk and could hear children singing, and farther away the endless, timeless noise of the sea breaking against the rocks.

Angus was standing on the steps leading up

to the massive front door, waiting for me.

"Come inside. We've got super rooms. Most of the other pupils are younger than us; abandoned children being coached to get into posh schools at huge cost – you know, the sort who wear suits, shorts and little jackets."

"Not the girls, surely?" I asked, laughing.

My room was fantastic, with views on both sides and one enormous bed in the middle.

"We are very lucky, the poor kids live in dorms on the top floor with Miss Pitcher in charge, a real old dragon with a moustache," my brother said. "Come across the passage and look at our bathroom; it's Victorian, with brass taps. How were the horses and what about Phantom?"

"He's all right. I hope I can look after him. I'm missing him already. I know it sounds crazy, but suddenly he doesn't seem mine any more," I said. "But what about the teachers? What are they like?"

"They are mostly young and a bit peculiar. The potter is a real weirdo," said Angus.

We met almost everyone later at tea in a large room overlooking the bay. Miss Pitcher kept the younger children in order. The girls wore skirts and blouses, the boys shorts and shirts. They were quiet and well behaved; they looked at me out of the corners of their eyes, and one of them muttered, "Is Phantom your horse? He's lovely." There were piles of scones, bread and butter, jam and biscuits.

Angus and I were introduced to a German called Hans, who was broad-shouldered, with fair hair cut short; to Jon from Poland who only spoke a little English; and to Jane who was large and blushed when she spoke to us. "I'm potting, what about you?" she asked, turning pink.

Potting? I thought frantically. Potting plants?

"She means making pots," said Angus. "Yes, I'm potting, Jane. Jean is riding. She's horse-mad, she can think of nothing else; it's a pity, but she's had the disease for many years now and we have to accept it's incurable."

"I'm sorry. Did you catch it from your horse?" asked Jane, not able to see the joke.

"Yes, from Phantom," I answered. "Sad, isn't it?"

"I won't have the pleasure of you in my class, then," said a young man with long hair, a beard and thick-lensed glasses hiding blue eyes. "I teach pottery. Won't you change your mind?"

I shook my head. "I won't have time. I want to learn stable management too. Horses are going to be my career," I said.

"I am going in for domestic science," announced Jane. "I like cooking and there's always work for anyone who can cook."

"I am going to be an engineer, to manage

engines, planes and the like," said Hans, looking at me. "They are better than horses. Is that
good English? Do I get it right?"

Mr Carli offered me a scone. He seemed to
be watching us all, summing us up, rather like a
tiger deciding which person to pounce on for
his dinner.

"How did you find Phantom, Jean?" he
asked. "Was he all right?"

"Super, thank you."

"What did you think of my Highland
ponies?"

"Very nice."

"Good foundation stock when I have my
stallion from Russia," he said, smiling at me.

I looked round the room. There were modern
pictures hanging on the walls, as well as two
which looked like old masters. Though everything looked perfect there was still something
missing. The scones were Scottish but the com-
pany wasn't, except for me and Angus who
were only half. And the house was so Scottish
that it needed its own people inside it.

"Who did all this belong to before?" I asked,
waving an arm around the room.

"Before I bought it? The old chief of the
MacInnes. He died and the death duties were
enormous. I got it for a very fair price," replied
Mr Carli in tones of tremendous satisfaction.

"So you are the laird now? Isn't that lovely,"

cried Jane, suddenly coming to life and then blushing.

"That's right, my dear. I am the new Laird of Uaine."

"And that is a good thing to be – yes?" asked Hans.

Miss Pitcher was driving her brood out of the room; she was thin and dry, without hope on her face; a woman waiting to retire, I thought. The sort of person who wears gloves in the summer out of habit.

After tea Angus and I wandered about the island. Phantom had been turned loose in a field with Lassie. They were already friends. He stood staring at the sea, his head high, his ears alert, his eyes shining, while the Highland stood behind him like a person in a queue. In a lower field someone had erected jumps and marked out a school.

Angus pointed to a flat strip of land where the grass was short and runways were marked out by strips of painted concrete. "That's the landing-strip – and what a perfect run in over the sea," he said.

"I hate airports. I think they eat up land and make fumes and noise. I would like us to go back to the horse age. I don't like cars either," I said, "so who cares?"

"You might if you had appendicitis and

needed a doctor in a hurry," retorted Angus.

"Look," I said, pointing, "another empty cottage. We've passed at least five in the last half hour. Where have all the people gone?"

"To make money. There are Scots doing just that all over the world," replied Angus. "Haven't you noticed?"

We walked to the jetty and looked at the boats.

There was a postbox which said NEXT POST TUESDAY and today was Friday. There was a telephone kiosk with the receiver ripped out, and a large bell which you could ring for the ferry, except that the ferry was no longer there.

"It's sad. It makes me want to cry," I said.

"It will come to life again. Think of the new breed of horse which will soon be here – the Carli breed," replied Angus.

"What do you think of the laird?" I asked.

"He's friendly, and he's got a super secretary called Maria with long legs and beautiful eyelashes," replied Angus. "What's your riding instructor like?"

"All right, so far," I said.

"My maths master is typical maths; just here for the summer. He's very nervous and he stutters. He had tea sent up to his room. I can't imagine him ever managing a class at our school, which is probably why he's here," said Angus.

There were sheep everywhere, unsheared, panting in thick coats, their square bodies supported by speckled legs. They walked like grannies with their big lambs running after them, baaing like overgrown infants.

We met a herd of wild Highland cattle too, with huge horns and long shaggy coats, their calves as woolly as teddy bears.

We sat on a rock and stared out across the bay where great shafts of sunlight lay on the sea. Everything was blue and gold.

"It's miles from home, isn't it?" I asked with a shiver.

"Yes, and lovely. I want to go out to inspect the lobster-pots," said Angus.

"If there are any lobster-pots," I answered.

"What's the matter? Don't you like it here?" asked Angus.

"Of course I like it. It's just that a month here seems a very long time."

"You'll be all right when you start riding and learning about splints and spavins; not to mention half a dozen dressage tests," replied Angus, laughing.

We returned to the house and almost at once Maria called us. "Telephone for you, Angus. It's your parents. You can take it in the office."

I seized the receiver.

"Are you all right?" asked Mum. "Do you like it? Is Phantom okay?"

"Yes," I shouted.

"It's marvellous," said Angus over my shoulder. "Wild, free and wonderful."

"It's so beautiful it makes you want to cry," I shouted.

"Wait till it rains," laughed Mum.

"How is the Middle East?" asked Angus, snatching the receiver.

"Hot," said Mum.

Then Dad came on the telephone and asked Angus about his maths. "Work!" he said. "I expect results, and that applies to Jean too."

"I'm going to," I answered, pushing Angus away. "I start tomorrow." Then suddenly the call was over.

"All right?" asked Maria, looking at us, and I noticed for the first time that the room was lined with filing cabinets, and furnished with a huge desk and swivel chair.

"Yes, thank you," I replied.

She followed us out, and, to my surprise, locked the door after her. "State secrets," she explained, laughing.

I looked at Maria and her eyes weren't with us; they were miles away seeing something else, and her hands were so tense that the knuckles showed white through her skin. I wanted to say, "What's the matter? Is something wrong?"

But at that moment she said, "Okay? Fine," and walked away smiling.

"She's strange, isn't she?" I asked.

"Oh, she's all right," said Angus. "I like her a lot. But then I like everything and everybody. I'm not suspicious and critical like you. I like it here."

"I like it too," I said, but I wasn't sure, not yet.

"There wouldn't be so many children here if it wasn't a super place. People don't send their children just anywhere," continued Angus. "It's expensive, too, and the teaching is of a very high standard. You should see the classrooms."

"No thank you. I prefer the stables," I said.

"You are so stand-offish, you really haven't met anyone yet," continued Angus. "There's a very nice Scottish girl called Janet, who's the cook – she's got a dear little baby, and two Spanish women who do the housework and help her in the kitchen. Do you know that the pottery teacher, Mr Smith, teaches five other subjects and so does my maths master, and that Maria teaches domestic science? Why don't you enrol for domestic science like Mum suggested?"

"For goodness sake, I have enough of lessons all term, and I plan to pass my maths exam next year. If I don't I'll think again," I said.

"There's a whole list of things hung up in the hall you can do. You haven't even looked at it," complained Angus.

"I don't want to. I want to forget school," I

35

said. "Next term will arrive soon enough."

"The Spanish women live somewhere at the back of the house; they don't speak English. I don't know their names yet," continued Angus. "The other children are all younger than us, which is a pity, and they don't do much besides endless French, Latin and maths – poor things. Listen, there's the gong for supper. I hope it's fish."

Later I climbed into my sumptuous bed. The sun was setting above the sea, burnishing it red and gold. The waves were lapping the white sand and somewhere in the sky a bird was calling. I'm glad I'm here, I thought. It's so beautiful, it's like a dream; and the sound of the waves became music as I slept.

3

How can I describe those first few days? They were beautiful beyond description, with the sea in the bay as calm as inland water and the rocks warmed by the sun. The school ran like clockwork with gongs and bells and scurrying feet. Angus did computer studies and made clay pots. The teachers nodded at me when they passed in the passage, but I stayed outside it all, determined only to ride. Caroline had her British Horse Society's Instructors Certificate. She had taught abroad and was a superb teacher, and I had her entirely to myself! It seemed like a gift straight from heaven, and I did not want to waste it.

I learned to sit deep in Phantom's saddle, to make him go as he had never gone before, with impulsion flowing from his quarters, his neck arched and proud, his jaw light and flexed. I learned to make the transitions from one pace to another as gentle and flowing as beautiful music until we seemed to glide together as one whole being, rather than rider and horse. I learned about navicular and ringbone, about tetanus and ragwort poisoning, about the theory of long reining and a great mass of stable management. I wrote it down on file paper from the office, thinking, I'll have it for life, if I forget anything I will still have my notes. When I was not studying or riding, I sat on the rocks and stared at the beautiful, calm, Highland sea and was sorry for the people in the prefabricated classrooms being stuffed full of maths, Latin and French.

I also thought about Caroline and wondered and pondered. She's too good to be here, I thought. She should be managing a stable with fifty horses and a covered school. She's like someone who has been hurt. Perhaps she is here to recover from something . . . maybe she was in love and going to be married and then jilted at the church gate. I wanted to ask her, to say simply, "What brought you here?" but it must be because of her father, I thought.

Jane was being coached for exams in November. Like Angus she had failed her maths. Her parents were separated and neither wrote nor telephoned. Jon was learning English, but spent much of his time studying the rocks on the island. He seemed to have no permanent home. Hans was learning English too; he seemed earnest and polite, the sort of person who always made his bed and never forgot to wash behind his ears. Sometimes he would sit on the rocks with me and tell me about Germany.

Days passed like this. Then one fine morning I hacked Phantom alone. Caroline watched me go, calling, "Stick to the tracks. Don't do anything silly," as though I was just a kid of nine or ten.

"Okay, don't worry," I called back over my shoulder, and then rudely, "I have hacked by myself before."

Everything seemed very still. There wasn't even a breeze, not a cloud in the sky, not a boat on the sea. I pretended the island was mine, that I was queen over everything – Queen of Uaine. Then I thought about the people, about how we had come from different parts of the world and all ended up on Uaine and how strange it was. Then I saw a cottage. Small and white, it stood by the shore. It was one storey with a simple thatched roof and two small windows and a door, nothing else. A terrier barked; there was smoke coming from a chimney and the smell of burning peat. Then a couple came outside and the man asked, "And who would you be? It is not often we have visitors."

"I'm Jean," I said. "And this is Phantom."

The man was young and bearded with a neat chin and red cheeks; the woman was young too, and pregnant. "Ian and Morag Macgregor," he

said. They held out their hands and we shook solemnly.

"Are you from the big hoose, then?" asked Mr Macgregor.

I nodded.

"A terrible place," said his wife. "Wicked to

be sure, as wicked as they come. That Mr Carli should be put away."

"I don't understand," I answered. "They've treated me all right."

"You will be paying though; money makes a difference," she said.

"He should never have had the place; the old laird looked after us all and the puir creatures too. Now the sheep are dying for want of care and the old people are all gone," said Mr Macgregor, patting Phantom. "But then money is the root of all evil and it is with money he bought the island, more's the pity, and now we are all done for, though why he wanted it I canna ken – but what do you know about such men, you so young . . .?"

"The school is good, it has good teachers," I said, "and it's lovely being here. But I must go now." I turned to leave.

"Aye, it's lovely all right," he called, "or it was before he came."

"I'm sorry," I shouted over my shoulder. "Very sorry."

On the way back I stopped to look at some goats cropping the peaty grass. They were heavily bearded and dirty white in colour, wiry, peaceful and unafraid. So all the people have gone, I thought. Mr Carli didn't want them. Only the Macgregors are left and she will have to go somewhere to have her baby. I pushed

Phantom into a walk again and started to think how Uaine must have been once, with the cottages full of islanders and perhaps the sound of bagpipes in the evening and the smell of smoking fish on the air; and children everywhere – Highland children. But there must have been bad things too, I thought, as we reached the square; no sanitation, the same old food week after week, cousins marrying cousins. Caroline was waiting for me.

"I met a couple in a cottage by the seashore," I said, dismounting. "They don't seem very happy."

"Ah, the Macgregors. They'll soon be gone," she said, running up my stirrups.

"Were there lots of people here when Mr Carli came?" I asked.

"About a dozen," she said. "They never paid any rent to the old laird, and their cottages were like pigsties. Father is going to get the best of the cottages done up and then we'll let them in the summer. But he did not turn out the people, they went of their own accord."

I didn't say anything as we brushed out Phantom's saddle mark together.

"Are you happy here?" asked Caroline.

"Yes, thank you," I said, but I wasn't sure. In spite of Mr Carli's efforts, the island seemed a sad place, as though secretly it was weeping for the days gone by.

Towards evening, the weather changed, flies swarmed in the bracken, midges hovered like moving clouds.

"I'm actually learning something," Angus told me, sitting in my sumptuous bedroom after dinner. "My maths teacher, Mr Matheson, is a really good teacher. He once taught at Eton. He's better than I thought."

"And I'm learning too," I answered. "I'm going to write to Mum and Dad tonight to tell them so."

"Excellent, then I needn't," replied Angus, laughing.

"All the same, I have reservations. I have a nasty feeling in my bones," I continued.

"Too much riding," Angus joked.

"I have the feeling that there's something wrong. I don't know why. I like Caroline, but like everyone else she seems to be under some sort of spell," I said.

"It's your imagination," answered Angus.

"Can't you feel it? Even Maria is not quite right. This house is like a stage set. We're all actors."

"Now I know you're mad," exclaimed Angus.

I stared out across the bay. A mile away lay Scotland.

"Everyone's gone except the Macgregors. The houses are empty. It's so sad," I cried. "There should be men fishing; the sheep should be sheared. It's all wrong somehow."

"Mr Carli has other plans. He wants to make this into an island paradise. This is only the beginning. By next year there will be chalets, rows of them, a caravan site perhaps, new stables. You know what he said; and change is never popular. I went up to the airstrip today. There are two three-seater planes there. I'm going to ask whether I can learn to fly," said Angus.

"It will go on the bill," I answered.

"I'll pay myself. I've got enough money. There's a hangar up there with a bigger plane inside; the one Phantom came in, fitted out for horses. Maria says it's for the Carli stud. She says they use it for flying in supplies, too. She gave me a drink last night, a Martini and soda," said Angus.

"You and Maria!" I exclaimed.

Mr Carli was crossing the bay in a speedboat, with foam lying like sudden snow in his wake.

"He's a playboy really," said Angus, looking over my shoulder. "Wouldn't you like to have all his money?"

"I don't know, but I do know that if I owned this island I would look after the sheep, the cattle and the people who were here before me," I said.

"Perhaps they didn't want to be looked after," replied Angus.

"I hate sitting next to him. He always asks about my riding. How was it today? Am I progressing? And Jane sits on the other side like a great lump of suet pudding staring at me with those huge, soulful eyes, wishing he would talk to her. It's awful!" I exclaimed.

"You're too sensitive," said Angus. "Try to like everyone, that's my motto."

"I'm going to study my book on dressage, then I'm going to bed," I told Angus. "I'm sorry, I'm probably just a bit homesick. I'll have a bath, that always cheers me up."

The bath water ran very slowly. By the time I was in bed it was dark outside. I think I fell asleep at once.

I dreamed I was in an aeroplane.

"All bale out . . . jump!" shouted a thin man with ginger hair.

"What about parachutes?" I asked.

"There aren't any. Grab anything heavy. Hang on to it," shouted a stout woman in a tweed skirt; then I was awake and Angus was standing over me in his pyjamas, saying, "Come and look, they are landing horses on the airstrip."

"It's a dream," I muttered, sitting up.

"It isn't. It's real."

I crept along the passage after Angus, floorboards creaking and moonlight dancing on the walls. Angus's curtains were drawn back and outside there was an aircraft and lights which had not been there before.

"It came in over the sea. I was awake. Then I saw the horses coming out, and I thought you would be interested." Angus picked up Grandpa's binoculars. "There's Caroline," he

said. "And Mr Carli and Maria and two strangers, one's a woman."

"Perhaps they are stallions and mares from Russia," I suggested.

"Oh, very likely! That plane couldn't fly more than a few hundred miles without refuelling," said Angus contemptuously.

"Anyway, it's none of our business," I said.

"They are leading them down the track to the square; they're out of sight now," Angus said, handing me the binoculars.

There was nothing to be seen but the hills and the lights being switched off on the airstrip.

"I hope I can ride them," I said.

I went back to bed, but I did not sleep. I heard the clock downstairs chime three. I heard Phantom neighing, and doors slamming and Mr Carli saying, "All right, Maria? Have a drink, George, you deserve it."

And I could find no reason for horses to be landed on the island at night, or only one – a need for secrecy.

At seven o'clock I dressed and ran down to the square. The main stable door was padlocked. Phantom had been turned out with Lassie in the lower meadow. There was no sign of Caroline. There were ships fishing far out in the bay. As I watched I saw Jacques bringing the ferry-boat into the jetty. Shortly afterwards he walked to the house, carrying a canvas bag,

his head bent against the wind. Suddenly the
hills seemed cold and barren and the grey sea
icy and without mercy.

I met Caroline as I walked back for breakfast. "What happened to the horses?" I asked.

"What horses?"

"The ones which came in the night."

She stared at me for a moment before she
answered. "They're in quarantine. They were
found to have something wrong with them. It
was either complete isolation or a bullet in their
heads, so they came here."

"Are they very infectious?" I asked.

"I don't know, but their vet came with
them," she answered. "They seem all right but
they have been in contact with a deadly virus."

"Poor things," I said. "How long will they be
here?"

"I don't know, one week, two weeks, it all
depends. See you later; we're going to work on
two tracks this morning," she said, "so I hope
you've done your homework."

"It's all right," I said when I met Angus on
his way to breakfast. "They're in quarantine."

"I know. Maria told me. We're to keep away
from them. Okay, Jean?" he asked. "Unless you
want Phantom to get it."

"They were going to be shot. I think Mr
Carli is jolly decent having them," I told him.
"Lots of people wouldn't."

"Exactly. He's a very nice man," said Angus. "And look, here's a postcard from Dad. Just to say they've arrived and Mum's writing. Someone must have been to collect the post."

"It was Jacques. I saw him," I said.

"By the way," Angus went on, "Maria's starting a shorthand class. She wants you to join. Jane has already started learning. Maria says you can always get a job if you know shorthand and typing."

"I know what I'm doing, I'm schooling horses," I answered. "I don't want any other job. Why don't you join the class, Angus?"

"She's teaching me chess," he said.

Breakfast was cereals, eggs and bacon, scones. Maria supervised us. Jane read a book as she ate. It was called *A Springtime of Love* by Faith Trance.

"Are you joining my class, Jean?" asked Maria, fresh and sweet-smelling in a summer dress and sandals.

"No, thank you. Isn't it exciting about the horses which arrived last night?" I asked. "When can we see them?"

"That is for Mr Carli to decide," she said. "But not for a day or two."

"Are they big or small? Hunters or ponies?" I added to help her along.

"I don't know. I don't know one end of a horse from the other."

"Well, what do they do? Horses do different things," I urged.

"Again, I don't know. I'm sorry, Jean. I'm not horse-mad like you," she replied, laughing.

"Surely I can see them from a distance?" I said.

"For goodness sake, Jean, it's nothing to do with me. Now eat up and get off to your lesson before you drive me round the bend," cried Maria.

I ran down to the square. Caroline had caught Phantom and tied him to a gate.

"No stable today?" I asked.

"That's right."

"When can I see them?"

"What?"

"The new horses."

"I don't know."

"What are they like?"

"I didn't see them properly. They were wearing rugs."

"But you must have seen them when you fed them this morning."

"I'm not saying, anyway. Hurry up and groom Phantom. Not the dandy-brush for his mane. How many more times have I got to tell you?"

"I can't wait to see them," I cried.

"All in good time."

I looked at Caroline and suddenly saw that

she was tired. Her hair hung in wisps around her face. Her eyes were ringed with dark shadows, her forehead creased in a perpetual frown.

"You don't seem very excited," I commented.

"Why should I be? I've seen enough horses to last me a lifetime," she said.

"Why did you come here then?" I asked.

"Because Father wanted me to," she said, and to my horror she started to cry.

4

"I'm sorry," I said, as she blew her nose. "I ask too many questions. Everybody says so."

"I just want you to remember that those horses are nothing to do with me, that bringing them here was Father's idea, not mine," said Caroline, sniffing. "If anyone asks you, I had no hand in it." In what? I thought, suddenly panic-stricken.

"Okay, now let's get on with your schooling," she said, while I thought: The horses are ill, they're going to die. Someone has been experimenting with some ghastly virus and it has gone wrong. I tried to school but my mind was in a turmoil and Phantom, sensing it, refused to walk. He jogged and threw his head up and down and sweated; he danced sideways and kicked at horseflies and broke a dressage marker. Caroline lost her temper.

"What's the matter with you both?" she cried. "Where are your legs, Jean? And just look at your hands. I said 'left rein, right leg'.

Are you deaf or something?" She seemed to be choking back tears as she shouted.

"Sorry. I *am* trying," I yelled.

"Stop and rest. Just stand and rest. I said *stand*," she shouted. "Don't you ever do what you are told?"

Phantom started to whirl round and round, and I could see Mr Carli coming down the long path between the rhododendrons. He swung his arms as he walked and his hair was swept back in its usual immaculate way.

"What's going on? It sounds like a fish market," he called.

"Nothing. It's my fault. I was being rude," I said, wanting to give Caroline time to compose herself.

"I don't like noise. I like tranquil surroundings," said Mr Carli, catching Phantom's reins. "I think I shall have to talk to you, Caroline."

I felt her cringe.

"It's my fault, I kept arguing. I think you're super taking all those horses on, Mr Carli," I hurried on. "I mean it would have been awful if they had been shot. You're what Dad would call 'a real brick'. Will they be in quarantine long?"

"I hope not. Now, no more noise please," he said. "And keep away from those horses, Jean. Understand? We don't know when they'll be in the clear. All right? I can trust you, can't I?"

"I hope so," I answered, wishing to keep my options open.

"So do I, because if your little horse gets it you'll be sorry," he said, walking on towards the sea.

"I can't teach any more," said Caroline. "I'm sorry. I've had bad news, terrible news. Go for a hack, dear, please, a quiet one and keep out of trouble, and please don't go far."

"Has someone died?"

"Yes, that's right, someone's died," she said, but I knew she was lying. "Keep away from trouble, Jean. Just ride round the tracks and then straight back here. All right?" I nodded. "You see, if you get into trouble, I shall. You understand, don't you?"

"Yes, of course."

"Thank you."

"I should go and have a sleep, or a really nice lunch," I said. "You'll feel better then, and afterwards I'll help you. I love mucking out."

I rode away along a rough track with bracken on each side, from which flies rose in their thousands and hung round Phantom's head like locusts. I felt in a daze, as though I somehow was ahead of time. I wanted to think. Caroline's face haunted me. Obviously the arrival of the horses had upset her. Were they about to die? Had she been consulted at all? Was she ever consulted about anything?

I started to trot as the road became smoother and passed an empty house, a deserted chicken run, an empty dog-kennel. Where is everybody? I wondered again. I could see the sea now, wilder today, angrier, throwing itself against sheer rock, withdrawing and trying again, battering the coast.

Tomorrow I will swim I thought, I will put on my bikini and sunbathe, and I will be nice to Caroline. After a time I turned back and met Caroline again by the square.

"We'll turn him out," she said, taking Phantom. "Sorry about earlier, please forget it."

"Can we ride together tomorrow? You could ride one of the Highlands," I suggested. "And I will ride Phantom."

"That's an idea. But first some stable management. I'm going to talk to you about teeth," said Caroline. "And then it'll be bits and martingales. Have you ever heard of a Wilson snaffle?"

Later, when I returned to the house, Angus asked, "What's happened? You look upset."

"Nothing's happened. I'm just tired." I did not want to draw Angus into my feelings, to have scorn heaped on them. I wanted to be alone. I lay on my bed, while rain drizzled from the sky, thinking: There's something wrong with this set-up. Maybe I'll visit the Macgregors. I'll try to find out what's going on. I knew it was against the rules, for we were not supposed to hack without special permission, and we had to tell someone where we were going. But Phantom was my horse, whether he rested or not was my business, and Dad was paying a fortune for us to be on the island. That's the way I saw it, anyway. So I felt no guilt when later I slipped down the narrow path to Phantom's field. He was wearing a headcollar and I had a piece of string. It was enough, because the tack room was locked and I would have had to ask someone for the key.

He whinnied when he saw me, and vaulting on to his sleek back I suddenly felt absurdly free. I felt the world was mine, which was ridiculous since Mr Carli owned the whole island and almost everything on it.

I thought of Dominic as I rode and wished he was with me, because he's the most sensible person I know and can cope with most situations. I imagined my parents in the Middle East and wondered what Mum was doing with herself all day long. Midges swarmed into my hair and stayed there. Horseflies hovered, then dived at Phantom like bombers. The sea was gentle again. It shimmered and, strangely, there was a swan swimming serenely alone.

Mr Macgregor was outside his cottage, leaning against the wall. He had a useless look

about him, as though he had given up hope of anything. "Good afternoon," I shouted. "Nice day."

"You could call it that," he answered, "and then again you could be calling it something else," he said deviously.

"How are you?" I asked. "And how is your wife?"

"Sad," he answered. "Aye, we're both sad. We will be leaving soon. This is no place to have a bairn, not now. Once we could have called the ferry when we needed it, but not since Mr Carli bought the island."

"I'm sorry."

"Aye, you mustn't be. It's not your fault, you seem a decent enough lass. We will be the last to go and it's awful lonely with none of your own kith and kin. It will be for the best, I'm thinking. Though it breaks your heart at times. Morag," he called. "We've got a visitor."

"It's guid of you to come," said Morag. "We don't see many people these days."

"Aye, and it's sad to see the animals now with no one caring, it's a shame."

"Isn't there anything anyone can do?" I asked.

"Nothing, unless you will be putting a bullet through Mr Carli's head."

"How do you keep in touch with your families?" I asked.

"We don't," replied Morag, "we canna. If we will be wanting a letter to go we have to take it up to the big hoose and who would be wanting to do that?"

"No one," I agreed.

"You're right there for sure."

Mr Macgregor started to pat Phantom. "He's a beautiful horse. Will you be hearing about the Australian horses?" he asked.

"What Australian horses?"

"It was on the radio this morning," he said.

I shook my head. "I've been busy. My brother brought a radio, but we haven't listened to it once," I answered.

"Och aye, you should always keep in touch," he said.

"Well, what about them?" I asked.

"They've gone, the lot of them. Kidnapped. The whole Olympic team. No one knows where they are, but someone is asking an awful lot of money for them – half a million pounds, was it, Morag?"

"What team? Where? In Australia?" I asked.

"In England, the whole Australian team of jumpers," replied Mr Macgregor. "They were training here, I believe."

"Including Milestone?" I cried. "Their top jumper, the horse who swept the board at Wembley last year?"

Suddenly I remembered how Dominic had

said that Milestone and his rider were to demonstrate to our Pony Club, that I would miss it . . . My mind started to race in circles.

"The papers would be full of it, I'm certain," continued Mr Macgregor. "Ask Mr Carli for a newspaper. He fetches one most days."

"Thanks for telling me. I must go now. I wasn't meant to come," I said, turning Phantom round, waving, thinking: The whole team! Milestone! One of the most famous horses in the world! How did they do it?

They *must* be in the square! I thought next. Right under our noses! Does Caroline know? She must, of course, I reasoned. She must be looking after them. That's why she looks so peculiar, she knows and disapproves, but can't let down her father. That explains everything.

A hard, icy ball of fear started to form in my stomach. What about the others? I thought. Not Jane, surely? I was sweating. I shall have to tell Angus, and we'll have to look at the horses, and then? Then what? Telephone the police when there was only one telephone, which was in Mr Carli's office? Catch a ferry to the mainland when every boat belonged to Mr Carli? Send out distress signals when we had none? I let Phantom go in his field.

"So you're back," called Mr Carli from behind the rhododendrons. "Have you forgotten the rules of this establishment?"

"No. I just felt like a ride," I answered brazenly, though inside I was quaking.

"I think we'll have to have a little talk, you and I," said Mr Carli. "Come to the office at six this evening."

He came through the rhododendrons, put an arm round my shoulder and said, "You must learn discipline. None of us like rules, but unfortunately our lives are governed by them and we don't want you growing up a law-breaker; what would your father say then, eh?"

"I don't know," I stammered.

"No hat, no bridle, you're not responsible for

your actions," he said. "Do you want a cracked skull?"

I shook my head.

"I will see you at six then."

He walked back to the house swinging his arms, while I stood gazing out to sea, my mind in turmoil. We must do something, I thought. We can't pretend it's not happening. Then I was running towards the house, rushing from room to room, looking for Angus.

"Whatever's the matter?" asked Maria, meeting me in a passage.

"Nothing. I'm looking for my brother."

"Well, you won't find him here. He's having a sailing lesson with Jacques. He'll be back for tea."

"A sailing lesson?" I cried.

"Yes. Whatever is the matter, Jean?" she asked.

"I've . . . I've just taught Phantom something rather special. I want to show the trick to Angus," I lied.

Quickly I pulled myself together. "Oh, er, Maria," I said, as she continued down the passage, "is there a newspaper I can read? I've finished my book and would like to read on my bed until teatime."

Maria stopped, her back to me. Then she turned and said coldly, "You know we don't get newspapers on Uaine, Jean. We haven't had any since last week. There are plenty of books in the library. Go and get one of those."

"But I saw . . ." I began, then gabbled on in a rush. "I mean thanks. Super. I'll go and look for one now." And I ran in the opposite direction before she could say anything more.

In the library, I sat in the nearest chair and tried to breathe normally. I had seen Jacques arrive with the post. Of course he had brought the newspapers. I knew Maria was lying.

5

"I don't believe it," cried Angus. "We know why the horses are here – it's crystal clear. You're just being alarmist." But I could already see his conviction wavering, he was not certain any more. "It simply can't be happening, not here, not with us."

"We'll have to see the horses. How will we recognise them?" I asked.

"That won't be difficult," he said. "There was a piece about them in *Horse and Hound* just before we left. And a picture. Hang on, I'm remembering." He stared out of the window. "There was the grey, Milestone, and a very large brown from Germany, and the others were big and wiry."

"Let's listen to the news on your radio," I suggested.

"It's still in my case." I found the radio and switched it on but no sound came.

"For goodness sake, what have you done? You are a fool, Jean, you must have broken it." Angus snatched it from me.

"Don't shout, they'll hear," I said.

"It's not definite, nothing is definite yet," said Angus, turning the knob on his radio.

"I'm scared. I don't know why, but I am," I said.

"Don't be stupid, they won't hurt us," he replied, opening the back of his radio. "I thought so, no batteries!"

"Who's the fool now! Fancy bringing it without any batteries!" I exclaimed.

"But I didn't," replied Angus.

"What do you mean?"

"Someone's taken them."

It really was the answer to our worst fears. It sent a tremble down my spine. "Are you sure?" I asked.

"Absolutely. I bought new ones specially for coming here. They cost me a fortune. I know I bought them, and I remember putting them in."

"So?" I asked.

"We are being watched. We are under suspicion. But I've got a camera with a film in it," said Angus. "So we can still take photographs as proof of the horses' identities."

The camera was empty too.

We looked at each other and I think we were both scared to the marrow of our bones.

"What about Jacques? Is he all right? Did you enjoy your sailing lesson?" I asked after a short, fraught silence.

"He's a communist. He doesn't speak much English. He knows his stuff though. We didn't talk much. He comes from a poor family – he hates the rich."

"And Mr Carli? Does Jacques hate him?"

"I don't know. But the horses. They were training in England for next year's Olympics."

"Where?"

"In the Cotswolds, near Princess Anne's place. It's incredible. How can they be here?" asked Angus.

"How many people know? Not Miss Pitcher, surely," I asked.

"Perhaps just Mr Carli. Perhaps he's fooled everyone else. He's clever. You can see it all over his face," said Angus. "And have you noticed how silently he walks? You turn round and he's behind you, and you haven't heard a thing."

"He must have accomplices," I said.

"Yes, the man and the woman who came in the night with the horses," replied Angus. "I didn't see them properly, but they were definitely there."

"And I heard Mr Carli offering the man a drink; he's called George," I said. "We'll have to make a plan. We'll have to see the horses and then go to the mainland for help. We can't handle it alone."

"But how do we get to the mainland?" asked Angus. "Why did it have to happen? Are they really so valuable? Just five showjumpers."

"But irreplaceable. It takes years to train a top showjumper, you know that," I said. "And Milestone is one of the best in the world. He holds the high-jump record. You must remember seeing him when we went to Wembley with the Pony Club!"

"The grey?" asked Angus.

"That's right, the grey." I was shaking all over now with fear and excitement. "We'll have to save them. The Australians will never pay, and if they don't Mr Carli will destroy the whole team," I cried.

"The one wearing a running martingale and a drop noseband . . .?" I nodded.

"Oh help," cried Angus. "I remember. He's a horse in a million!"

"That's right, irreplaceable," I repeated.

"But how did they do it?"

"We don't know yet," I said.

I sat on Angus's bed, while he sat on a chair, his head in his hands. "The Australians might simply pay up," he said hopefully. "Then the horses will be saved."

"But what if they refuse?" I cried. "We've got to do something."

"There must be someone who will help," said Angus after a while. "Let's wait a bit and work things out."

"How long do you think we've got?" I asked.

"Days, weeks. I don't know. More than hours anyway," said Angus.

Later I saw Mr Carli in his study. Angus wanted to be with me. "Two heads are better than one," he said.

"I don't want to look suspicious. I want to play it cool," I told him. "He's not likely to kill me."

"Not yet," muttered Angus.

"Don't be silly."

I knocked on the door. Mr Carli was sitting at his desk. He looked like any other headmaster. Suddenly I wasn't frightened any more.

"Sit down," he said, pointing to a chair. "Now be silent for five minutes and consider your behaviour." I sat down and looked round the office. Once it had been a room where people had laughed and talked, perhaps children had even played there, or the old laird had used it for his gunroom. Now it was like a million other offices, cold and functional.

"You must have had a job bringing all this stuff over," I said, waving airily at the office equipment.

Mr Carli raised a tanned hand on the end of a hairy arm. "I said, Silence," he shouted.

I thought of my parents: If only they could see me now, I thought. Of Dominic milking his cows, swilling down the cowhouse, turning off the lights. I thought of our help, Mrs Parkin, picking up the post in Sparrow Cottage. It seemed a long way off. Will we ever see it again? I thought. And then, Don't be melodramatic, Jean.

"Right, is your mind clear now?" asked Mr Carli, beckoning me over to his desk and looking me straight in the face.

"As clear as it will ever be."

"I wish to impress upon you the consequence of breaking the rules on this island, which are made, I might say, for the good of all. If you continue to trespass on the island, we will have to confiscate your horse. Lock him up. Is that clear, Jean?" he asked.

"You can't, he's mine," I said.

"But you're here on my island, and under my control," retorted Mr Carli.

"Being paid for, as a pupil," I insisted.

"I am not going to argue with you, Jean. I just wish you to understand that it is for your own good and safety to obey the rules."

He stood up. The interview was at an end.

But the threat was there. Phantom was to be the pawn in the game.

"No hard feelings." His arm was round my shoulder again. It was thick and hairy and smelled of suntan lotion.

"No," I said.

Angus was waiting for me outside. "Well?" he asked.

"Nothing much," I answered as we walked down the stairs together. "I'm going to visit those horses tonight. Will you come too?" I whispered.

"I don't know. Can't we just forget all about it?" asked Angus.

"No we can't," I said. "Can't you see how important it is? Let's go outside in the fresh air. I can't breathe in here, and supposing it's bugged?"

"Don't exaggerate," replied Angus. "We've got to stay calm."

Dinner was a strange meal. Mr Carli made amusing conversation to me as though our interview had never happened. Jane upset her water and Mr Carli opened a bottle of wine. I felt all the time as though I was sitting on a time bomb, and because of that it was impossible to concentrate. And the wine made me silly so that soon I could do nothing but giggle.

After dinner we played cards and I lost every hand.

"I should go to bed, Jean, the wine must

71

have gone to your head," said Maria, winking at Mr Carli.

The stairs moved as I walked up them, the walls swayed. I lay on my bed and the ceiling went round and round. After a time I slept and dreamed that Phantom was lying dead on the seashore.

I woke up to find that I was still fully dressed and that dawn was breaking across the bay, the most beautiful dawn I had ever seen. And I knew now what I must do. There was no other way. I had to see the horses in the square.

I woke Angus, "I'm going to the square," I said. "Are you coming with me?"

He was still dressed too. "That wine was like poison," he answered, sitting up. "Of course I'm coming with you."

We crept down the wide front stairs and opened the enormous front door. I could hear my heart beating as loud as the sounding of a drum. The grass was wet with dew. The sun rising above the sea had made a path of palest gold across the shimmering water. The wild goats had appeared in the night and were grazing near the square. Their long beards made them look like old men.

We tried the gates to the square but they were padlocked. "There's a window at the back of the stable," I said. "We can push it open and then climb in."

"I feel as though there should be a search-light, as though we were in a prison camp," said Angus.

"Same here."

We were both shivering, half cold, half fear.

"Are you sure you've got it right? Half a million pounds is a lot of money," said Angus, as we waded through nettles.

"A hundred per cent," I answered, because now everything was clear-cut and certain in the bright morning light. It all added up.

The window was higher than I thought. The nettles stung through our jeans, and we were seized by panic when we thought we heard a voice, but it was only a nanny-goat calling to her kid. We dragged boulders to the window, stinging our hands on the nettles. We piled them on top of one another, while inside a horse whinnied.

"They're tranquillised, of course," said Angus.

"I wonder where George is now."

"Gone back, I expect."

"Or lying low somewhere."

"I wish there were more of us," I said, climbing on to the boulders.

"Perhaps your friends the Macgregors will help," suggested Angus.

"Yes, I think they will." I was hanging on to the windowsill.

Angus pushed more boulders under my feet.

"I hope we are wrong," he said. "I don't want to be a hero. I want to have a nice peaceful holiday and pass my maths exam."

The window opened inwards. Cobwebs clung to my hair.

"Don't frighten the horses," said Angus. "Drop down gently. Careful now."

"Shut up, just shut up," I answered, and then I was landing on a bed of peat. I stared at the hocks in front of me and prayed that their owner would not kick.

"All right? Is everything all right?" Angus called. "Can I jump now?"

"Wait a minute. Hang on."

The horse had a fiddle face, a drooping lower lip, a narrow cheek. He was brown and wiry and dressed in a quilted rug. He was half asleep and the whole stable smelled like a vet's surgery.

"Okay, jump," I said.

"What about the horse?"

"He's drugged."

Another second and Angus was beside me, dusting his knees.

In the loose box next door, a chestnut lay on the peat, his hoofs tucked neatly under him.

"Do you recognise any of them?" I asked anxiously.

"Not yet," said Angus.

"It's like Madame Tussauds, they're like dummies," I moaned, patting a brown neck.

"Look, look next door but one, it's Milestone," cried Angus. "The grey with the big sleepy ears, and the huge eyes. I would recognise him anywhere. You're right, it is them!"

"But how?" I cried. "How did they pull it off?"

"We don't know, do we? We may never know, but it's them all right," said Angus.

"What are we going to do?" I asked.

"Save them, of course."

"But how?"

Milestone was standing with his head hanging low. He wasn't interested in us; none of them were, they were barely conscious. I patted his dark grey neck, spoke to him, but it wasn't any use. "It won't take much to kill them, will it? Because they're half dead already," I said.

We didn't recognise the other two horses, but we knew it was the Australian team. It was not a nice discovery.

"We must make a plan," said Angus at last. "It's no good moping here. Let's go."

I kissed Milestone goodbye. "We'll save you, don't worry," I promised. "We won't forget you."

I imagined a horse box in a country lane with stone walls on each side. A gang flagging it down on some pretext or other, knocking out the driver and the groom, driving away, abandoning the horse box, transferring the horses to

76

another, then, somewhere, on some lonely dis-
used airstrip, loading them on to Mr Carli's
plane.

I imagined the Australians waiting for their
horses to arrive. Pacing up and down a show-
ground, waiting in the stands, telephoning. Or
were the horses kidnapped on the way home?
We might never know. They were large, slightly
battered horses, accustomed to travelling, and, if

they argued, there was always a tranquilliser. I wondered what the ransom note had said. It must have caused a stir. I imagined how the Australians must feel with their whole team gone. How I would feel in the same situation?

It was something too big for us to handle; but whom could we ask for help? Miss Pitcher? Jacques? Mr Matheson? The pottery teacher? Were they all in it too, like Maria? Who would it be safe to ask?

"We need help," I said.

"That's the understatement of the year. But who is there?"

"I don't know. But there must be someone," I answered. "Can we steal a boat?"

"They're all padlocked."

"Isn't there a rowing-boat?"

"The oars are locked in the boathouse," said Angus. "Jacques has got the key. Quickly, Jean. Let's get out of here. If we're caught, we're finished."

A few minutes later we were blinking in the early morning light outside.

"We could cable our parents," I suggested.

"How?" asked Angus.

"I don't know."

"You know we can't, so we must make a plan. We'll have our lessons as usual and then after lunch we'll go and call on your friends the Macgregors."

"They're leaving soon," I interrupted.

"Give them a message, and they can ring the police," said Angus.

"Yes, but they must be quick. I'm afraid for Phantom, and it would be awful if they killed Milestone. It just doesn't bear thinking about," I said.

"There's no other way," said Angus.

"Yes, I hope they're reliable, that's all," I muttered. "Supposing Morag starts having her baby?"

"We'll have to risk that. Now let's go back to bed again," said Angus.

"Do you think we can make it?"

"Of course."

We slipped through the front door and locked it again after us. I could hear my heart thumping as we crept up the wide, rather splendid staircase to our rooms. I lay on my bed and thought, and, whichever way I reasoned, I knew that nothing would be easy, that there was no easy way out. Then I imagined the Australian horses being killed one by one, and I knew that we had to go on, that we had to fight to the bitter end to save them.

Soon I could hear voices outside on the lawn. Mr Carli was giving Caroline orders, and in the dining-room the tables were being set for breakfast.

It was like any other day, and yet completely

different. I couldn't imagine how it would end, how we would ever outwit Mr Carli, who could kidnap a whole team and fool the British police force. But if we failed and the horses were killed, I knew that Milestone's huge eyes would haunt me for the rest of my life.

6

"We're playing games this afternoon," said Mr Carli, smelling of aftershave, at breakfast. "The road is being blasted and I don't want anyone hurt. What game shall it be?"

I caught Hans staring at me. Was he trying to say something? Warn me? How much did he know? Could we trust him?

"Come along now, let's have an answer," continued Mr Carli.

"Rounders, I suppose," suggested Angus.

"Netball," cried Jane, her face scarlet because she had actually voiced an opinion at last.

"Something simple, please," said Hans.

"My ankle is not too good, I'll stay upstairs," I answered.

"Come, Jean, you are skiving. If your ankle hurts you must be umpire. I will let you blow the whistle. You always have something to say. You will do very well," said Mr Carli, laughing.

"No thank you," I cried, imagining Caroline killing Phantom while we played rounders.

"Miss Pitcher will bring her charges; it will be a great game. I shall be first to bat," continued Mr Carli.

I finished my toast and marmalade and made for my bedroom.

"Don't give the game away," said Angus, following me upstairs. "Play it cool. You look at your wits end."

"I am. I keep imagining the horses in a mass grave with Phantom on the top," I hissed.

"Think positive," said Angus.

Phantom was ready for me.

"You look in a state, Jean. What's the matter?" asked Caroline.

"Nothing."

"Your boots are on the wrong feet. Are you all right?"

"Yes, of course."

"You don't look it."

"Well, I am," I said, changing my boots round.

I trotted in circles, improved my transitions, but suddenly it was all pointless. What did transitions matter compared with the predicament of the horses in the square?

"You're not attending," complained Caroline after a time. "Sit deeper in your saddle, use your back."

I hated her voice now – everything about her. She was nothing but a traitor, a criminal, and yet she was the best instructor I had ever had.

"Walk," she called. "Relax." I let my reins go slack.

The hills were very grey, green and brown. Somewhere there must be help. I will go to the Macgregors, I decided – now.

"I'm going for a ride. I can't concentrate. We're both bored stiff, can't you see?" I cried, turning Phantom's head towards the sea.

"You will do as you're told," cried Caroline. "Father is quite right, you're an undisciplined hooligan."

A breeze straight from the sea hit my face. The air smelled of salt. Phantom's hoofs thudded on the rough path. Sheep fled like grannies, calling to their young. Goats stared at me like wise old men, while Caroline called, "Come back. Come back at once, Jean."

The sea was still washing the shore, its foam like detergent on the sand between the rocks. A man was standing by the Macgregors' cottage, smashing the windows slowly and methodically.

"Where are they?" I asked, trying to keep my voice steady as the panic rose inside me.

"Gone and good riddance," he answered.

"Why are you doing that?" I asked, my voice trembling with shock.

"So they won't come back."

He was English and swarthy, and somehow I knew he was George, and dangerous.

"Later I am going to blow it up. Want to watch?" he asked.

"But their things are still inside. Can I take their things to them, please," I cried. But I knew already that it was too late, that we should have visited them before breakfast, that our last contact with the outside world had gone.

George shook his head. "I shouldn't interfere," he said. "You don't want to be in trouble with the guv'nor, do you?"

"Why can't things be left alone? This was a happy place once," I cried.

"How do you know? Been here before have you?"

I shook my head.

George looked as though he had been in prison. His hair was short, his face leered when he looked at me. His hands were scarred, large and knotted, his feet encased in army-type boots. His clothes hung on his large frame, an odd, city-like suit, obviously second-hand.

"There's nothing worth anything inside, just old furniture and pots and pans. It's no place to bring up kids. It should have been condemned years ago. There isn't an inside toilet, no electricity, not even a cooker; they must have lived like pigs. The sooner it's razed to the ground the better," he said, kicking at the walls.

It was inconceivable that he and the smooth

Mr Carli should be friends, and yet they were. I wondered if Mr Carli had been in prison. Surely not, with such beautiful manners.

"Have you known Mr Carli a long time?" I asked.

"What, the boss? Long enough."

Phantom was pawing the ground.

"You're friends, anyway," I insisted.

"You could call us that."

"And you are enjoying smashing up the cottage? What a pity," I said.

"It ain't fit to live in. I've told you. And you watch your step, young lady, or you'll be in trouble. I'm warning you . . ."

I turned away.

Caroline was not to be seen when I reached the square. I slid to the ground, untacked Phantom, and turned him out in the long field near the house. I knew I was in for trouble. I had broken all the rules and knew too much, but surely there must be someone who can help, I thought, walking towards the house, someone honest somewhere.

I was late for lunch. When I entered the dining-room, Mr Carli was saying grace:

"For what we are about to receive, may the Lord make us truly thankful." It was as false as everything else – just part of the act he was performing as headmaster. He frowned at me as I sat down.

"Late again, Jean," he said.

"Sorry. I was watching someone smashing windows," I answered, unfolding my napkin.

"You see too much," he said. "You would be better to stick to the rules which are made for your own good."

We ate stewed lamb, ice cream, raspberries. It all tasted the same to me because I was still seeing Milestone standing in his loose box like someone drunk. Every minute spent eating was suddenly a waste of time. Hans did not look at me, nor did Angus; only Jane kept catching my eye and smiling as though she knew I was in disgrace and was trying to cheer me up. I tried to smile back, but thinking of Milestone froze my face, and I felt tears pricking behind my eyes. I stared out of the window. The bay was empty, cold and grey, offering us no hope of any kind.

"Your ankle seems to have recovered," said Mr Carli, standing up. "Are you going to play rounders?"

I shook my head.

"You can stay in your room, then," he said, exasperated.

"Thank you."

We trooped out. The hall smelled of furniture polish.

"See you," muttered Angus between his teeth.

I sat on my bed and tried to make a plan,

but my mind was tired for want of sleep and all I could see was failure. If only we had been in time, I thought. If only I had given the Macgregors a message, we might already be saved; the Australian horses might be on their way home; Mr Carli in handcuffs; but we were too late. And on such mistakes battles are lost, horses die and we may all perish. I was trying not to cry when I heard a knock on the door and a voice asking, "May I come in?"

It was Hans, clean and smiling. Jumping off my bed to face him, I thought, Friend or foe?

There were dark shadows under his eyes which had not been there before. He looked older and sadder, though his eyes were as blue and clear as the sea outside.

"What do you want? You should be playing rounders," I said. My voice had changed too; it was higher than usual and it trembled at the end, like an engine about to break down.

"I want to ask you something. There is no one else I can ask," said Hans.

"You had better sit down then," I suggested.

He sat on a chair, his large hands hanging uselessly on each side of him.

"Asking you is a risk; everything is a risk in this place," he said.

"But you have to take it," I said. "Is it about some horses?"

His face lit up. "Yes, and you know about horses. That is why I come to you," he said.

"They came in the night?" I asked cautiously.

"Yes."

"Well, what is it you really want to know about them?" I asked.

"I want them identified."

Suddenly I knew it was all right. It was as if a huge weight had been removed from my chest.

"They are . . . " I said, "they are the kidnapped team, including Milestone."

"I thought so. I have heard about it on the

radio, but I had to be sure. They are from Australia. Right?"

"Right," I said. "But where do you come in?"

"It is a long story," replied Hans, smiling, "and I should be playing rounders."

"So we are on the same side?" I asked.

"Yes, we always have been. I like you and your golden horse. I trust you. Nothing must happen to you. We must be careful."

"What are we going to do?" I asked, standing up and going to the window. "We wanted to send a message to the mainland, but now even the Macgregors have gone. How did you know anyway? Have you still got a radio?"

He shook his head. He reminded me of Dominic for he was calm in the same way.

"There is a radio in the kitchen. I go there in the evenings to listen with Janet. She is a nice girl. She is the only Scots person left. She stays silent because of her baby, but she is on our side."

Suddenly I remembered the school's cook, whom I had only seen once or twice. Angus had told me about her. I could feel hope returning. "Why did you come here, Hans?" I asked.

"It is a long story. I will tell you some other time. Now I must go. Tonight we will listen together, we will decide what comes next." He took my hand suddenly, pressed it quickly, then shut the door quietly after him. I lay on my bed, listening to the game of rounders below. If this room is bugged, I thought, Mr Carli will know everything, and then we'll all be finished, but Hans did not say anything about bugging so it was probably all right. Outside on the lawn Jane laughed.

Mr Carli shouted, "Well caught. Keep it up," in his hearty headmasterly voice.

But if Hans is really on Mr Carli's side, we might as well be dead, I thought, all of us in a joint grave, the horses, Angus and me, or maybe they'll ransom us too. Then, without warning, I fell asleep.

7

Evening came and went as I slept. I wakened to find the sky darkening into night outside. My first thought was – Phantom! I rushed to the door, turned the handle, pulled, threw my weight against it. It wouldn't budge. I saw them murdering Phantom as I struggled. Then I ran to the window. The drop was six metres or more, straight on to stone steps. I was trapped.

Then I heard Angus talking through the door.

"It's all right, Jean," he whispered. "Everything is under control."

"What about Phantom?" I whispered back.

"He's all right, I've just looked. He's grazing quite happily."

My panic subsided. But for how long would he be safe? I wondered. How long before Mr Carli took his revenge and taught me a lesson? "Hans is on our side," whispered Angus.

"I know," I whispered back.

"Just hang on. We're going to get you out later and then we'll listen to Janet's radio and make a plan," whispered Angus, and was gone.

It was agony waiting; terrible thoughts rushed through my head with the speed of an express train, frightening images rose before my eyes. Time seemed to pass at the pace of a caterpillar clambering across a cabbage leaf. Everything seemed abnormally quiet and still, like the lull before a storm. Soon the hills were completely wrapped in darkness, with no moonlight to give one hope. I felt shut in then, more than I have ever felt before. In spite of the electric light I felt as though I was in a black hole from which I would never emerge. I had no watch and the sky told me nothing except that dawn was still hours away.

Then at last I heard a noise in the room next door and Angus's voice saying, "We're just moving a wardrobe, there's a door behind it. Don't worry, everything is going to be all right." He muttered the words through his teeth as though holding something in his mouth. Then I whispered again, "What about Phantom?"

"He's all right. He's all right till morning anyway," whispered Angus. "Move your wardrobe, will you? There's a papered-over door on the other side of it."

I struggled and pulled and slowly edged the wardrobe away from the wall, revealing the outline of a door. The paper started to wobble and then to tear as a screwdriver poked through it.

A second later Angus and Hans appeared, smiling.

"So?" exclaimed Hans.

"What's the time?" I asked.

"Nearly midnight. We go to the kitchen now," said Hans. "Hurry or we will miss the news. Your little horse is all right, Jean, I promise. Do not worry, and stop shivering."

The floorboards creaked.

"We'll go down the back stairs. Follow me," said Hans.

The kitchen was old-fashioned, with an Aga and a Welsh dresser, a great stone sink and wooden plate racks, and a scullery next door.

"These are my friends, Janet," said Hans. "Angus and Jean. They know everything. Jean is starving."

Janet held out a small plump hand. She had hazel eyes and was wearing a pinny over a brown skirt and blouse.

"Don't make a noise, or you will be waking the baby," she said, taking my hand. "Sit yourself down."

"It's good of you to have us here," I said, while Hans fiddled with a radio and Angus paced the kitchen like a horse waiting for a race.

The radio came on.

"I feel like someone in a war," said Angus.

"Yes, but this time we're on the same side," replied Hans.

"What about the light? Won't Mr Carli be suspicious?" I asked.

"Och aye, he'll think it's the baby waking," replied Janet, "and I am glad to have you. It is awful lonely here on my own. I would leave tomorrow if I had somewhere to go. I'll be getting you something to eat while you're listening, Jean. It is a terrible business – all those puir horses. It's time Mr Carli was found out. I'm thinking . . ."

"Shhh. Shut up," said Angus. "Listen!" He sat down at the table with us.

The radio was old and crackly. It must have been in the kitchen for years and because of that no one had thought of gagging it. It was like the dresser and the sink, part of the furniture, and because of that no one had noticed it.

The announcer was talking about the horses. He said there were no new leads, that the police were still looking for a green horse box, and for a tall, swarthy man. He said that the police were particularly interested in tracing the grey horse called Milestone and anyone seeing strange horses in their vicinity should get in touch with the police at once. He said that an international gang was involved and that the horses might now be in Europe. I think we were all shaking with excitement when he eventually stopped talking about the kidnap.

"It really is unbelievable," I gasped. "And they think they're in Europe."

"The Australians are not paying; they make no mention of paying," said Hans.

"Och aye, they'll never pay," said Janet.

"Why are you here, Hans? Why did you come?" asked Angus, switching off the radio.

Hans rubbed his nose and looked at us.

"You can trust us," I said, and I knew suddenly that he had been waiting for this moment for a long time.

"To settle old scores," he said.

"What old scores, Hans?" I asked.

"I think he killed my father."

I said nothing for a moment, because it seemed too awful to think about.

"How?" asked Angus.

"By accident. They were on a building site. Carli was on the crane. He let it fall – a load of bricks . . ." replied Hans.

"But why?" I asked.

"Because my father knew too much. He knew about the protection racket. He was going to the police. After that Mr Carli vanished."

"You're not a secret agent, are you?" asked Angus, sounding impressed.

"No. I am too young."

"What about the other people here?" I asked.

"I don't know. I don't trust any of them, not completely. They may have secrets too," said Hans. "Mr Carli has been here for two years. He has been keeping quiet. He was called something else before. He has had several names. Maybe this kidnap is his last big scoop . . ."

"You mean 'was'. We are going to save the horses," said Angus. "He's not getting away with it this time."

"He is very clever. Someone sent me his photo; it appeared in a paper here advertising this school. I knew his face; the scar gave him away."

"Why didn't you tell the police?" Angus asked.

"Because nothing was proved. It looked like an accident. I am the only one who remembers, and my mother. We knew it was not an accident. I think he is running out of money. The school has not been the big success he hoped, so now the kidnapping; the holding to ransom. It is all very clever, yes? Who would think of the horses here. Who but you two who came by chance and know horses? And me who is on his tail?"

"You speak good English," I said.

"I have studied it for a long time. But now we must save you and your horse, Jean. It is our first task," said Hans.

"Supposing we pretend to have appendicitis? Angus could. They would have to send him to the mainland," I suggested.

"I think he would not be sent," said Janet simply.

"What's on the other side of the island? Hang on, I've got a map. I found it in the office when the door was open. It's just a photocopied piece, but it's enough," said Angus, searching his pockets.

I leaned over his shoulder. "There must be another side to an island," I suggested.

"Brilliant," said Angus.

"It's eight miles to the other side and then

there is Tuath – that will be nearly a mile across the sound," Janet told us.

"Is it inhabited?" asked Angus.

"Och aye."

"Are there telephones?"

"Aye, of course."

"Jean can go," said Hans.

"What, eight miles and then swim a mile? I can't. I tell you, I can't do it," I said.

"But Phantom can. You can ride him, and he can swim. It is possible," said Hans.

"You swim better than I do. Look, there are little islands in between where you can stop and rest, and we must stay and guard the horses," Angus argued.

"And sabotage the planes," said Hans.

"When do I go?" I asked.

"At low tide," answered Hans. "There's a chart of tides by the boathouse."

"It is a long way over the hills," said Janet. "Right over the top and awful steep on the other side."

"And then rocks?" I asked.

"There's a sandy bay," she said. "White sand, you canna miss it. I played there as a child. White sands and seals with their pups."

"It sounds like heaven," said Angus.

"You had better keep the map, Jean," said Hans, putting it into my hand. "We won't be going far."

Looking at him I suddenly saw how tense he was. Janet was making us coffee.

"Here ye are," she said, handing us each a mug. "You must be keeping up your energy."

We drank our coffee in silence. I was seeing the white sand, the seals and the swim which lay ahead, while Hans turned a signet ring round and round on the third finger of his right hand, and Angus gnawed at his nails.

"Now we'd better go back to bed," Angus said, "and try to sleep."

We took our mugs to the sink.

"No one suspects me. I will go to the boat-house in the morning and look at the charts," said Hans.

"Now we'll put the wardrobes back – and then shall we meet after lunch tomorrow?" asked Angus. "Take the number Dad gave us, Jean."

"Yes. I think," I said slowly, "I'll go after lunch. Unless something else crops up. If Phantom is in danger I shan't wait. Thank you for everything, Janet."

We crept back to our rooms – I went back through the door behind the wardrobe, and pushed it back to hide the damaged wall. I climbed into bed and was suddenly homesick. I longed for our cottage, for the small windows, for the orchard, for the safety of being at home, for the beech-woods and the long straight track

to Dominic's farm, and the sound of the commuter traffic starting up in the morning; even
that. Suddenly the silence in my room seemed to
dominate everything. I put out the light and
slowly dawn came, with the cheerful chatter of
birds. I must have slept then, for I was woken
by the sound of giggling outside.

A voice squeaked, "You've overslept. Breakfast is almost over. I thought you would like to
know." More giggling came from outside the
passage.

"Thank you," I shouted. "What's the time?"

"Nine o'clock, time for lessons. Quick! Run!
Miss Pitcher's coming."

Suddenly I wished I was their age, just eight
or nine, with no real worries. I tried my door. It
was not locked any more.

Then I remembered Phantom. I pulled back
the curtains. Mist lay over the bay, thicker than
muslin. I pulled on jeans and a tee shirt, and
rushed downstairs.

Hans was standing by the window. "It is
misty, is it not?" he asked.

Suddenly the night before seemed like a
dream. "Is everything the same?" I asked.

"Yes, nothing is changed."

I helped myself to a boiled egg.

"You are late. Lessons have started. The big
man will be angry," said Hans.

"I'm scared. I wish I was going now," I

muttered. The thought of what lay ahead hung over me, heavy as a storm about to break.

"You will be all right. We will win. But you must eat," said Hans.

"Where's Angus?"

"Learning his maths."

"I'll go before lunch," I muttered. "Tell them I went riding. They can think I'm lost. It will be better that way." I forced a scone into my mouth, not tasting it.

"What about Angus?" asked Hans.

"Tell him I couldn't wait, okay?"

Hans looked straight at me as though his eyes could give me courage.

"All right, and the best of British luck," he said.

I changed into jodhpurs and found Caroline waiting for me in the square.

"Would you like to jump? I've put up some new fences," she said.

"Super," I said, running down my stirrups.

Were her hands shaking while she helped me? Or did I imagine it? I thought I read anxiety on her face, and that her voice was strained. "Right. We'll start with the cavaletti," she said. The mist had vanished. The sea was calm and blue-green. Phantom jumped beautifully. Caroline corrected my leg position, told me to measure my strides as I approached each fence and talked about ground lines. I tried to

concentrate, but all the time I was imagining Tuath, seeing myself on the other side of the sound, riding for help.

"Right, once more. Off you go," Caroline called. The course was about three feet high. There were only five fences. Phantom flew over them as though they weren't there, as though they were nothing.

"He can certainly jump," said Caroline. "What would you like to do next?"

"Can we have a little hack? Just to cool Phantom down," I suggested.

"If you promise to be good."

I nodded, suddenly unable to speak.

"Don't go far," she continued, looking at her watch. "Be back by twelve-thirty."

"All right. Thank you, thank you very much," I said, turning Phantom, wondering whether I would ever see her again.

"Remember to walk the last bit home," she said.

"Sure," I shouted. "I won't forget."

8

I had left the map behind but I had in my hat the special telephone number we can always use if we are in trouble. I knew the way was straight over the hills, up and then down to the sea. It seemed simple enough. Phantom walked with a long swinging stride, while I suddenly felt courageous, like someone in a war crossing the enemy lines. I even sang a little and thought of my parents in the Middle East. There should be troubles out there, I thought, but instead it's Angus and me who are having the adventures.

I imagined telling Dominic all about it when I was home again. I saw him leaning on a fork, a little bovine like his cows, listening. I'm living, I thought, and I'm going to save the horses and let the Australians see there are still people of courage in Britain. I sang pop songs and songs from shows.

The sun was hot on my back, Phantom was sweating and the path was still uphill. I turned in my saddle and I could see the bay far below, so I knew I was still on the wrong side of the island. The path was very steep, and suddenly I felt vulnerable and was glad that Phantom was not grey, that he blended so well with the yellowing bracken. Birds wheeled over us, dipped and were lost above the sea. If Mr Carli looks through binoculars he can see me quite clearly, I thought, but why should he look through binoculars? I started to whistle. Sheep moved out of our way, panting in their thick coats. Two goats peered at us from behind a boulder. The path still wound up and up, and the bay was still behind us, empty and clear, far, far, below. When we are at the top we'll see the other side and Tuath, I thought. I shall start singing again then, and there will be only the downward path ahead, and then the swim . . . We crossed some peaty ground. Phantom stopped to drink, sucking the dark water from the wet grass as though it were wine.

"Nearly there," I said, "just a few more strides and we'll be looking down on Tuath."

I dismounted and squelched through the peat, until the top of the hill became a plateau and beyond lay another hill. I sat on a rock and rested.

"It doesn't matter. We've still got plenty of time," I told Phantom. "Not to worry."

Brave words, because inside I was beginning to quake and there was a funny feeling down my spine. A small voice was asking: 'Supposing you never reach the other side? What then?'

I shook myself and Phantom shook himself too. Then I mounted and rode on.

We crossed the plateau and started to walk downhill. Flies swarmed above our heads. The path was steep so I led Phantom, and my hair stuck to my head with sweat while I wondered what the time was, how long we had been travelling, how much time there was left?

Phantom slipped and slid, his nylon girth was sticky with sweat, his sides dark with it. We reached the bottom and started to climb again, wading through bracken which seemed as endless as a prairie.

"Not far now," I told him. "We'll get cool in the sea. Not to worry."

Flies bit us both, deer fled from us, leaving a path through the bracken. I should have waited, I thought, found out the tides and the time. I should have brought food, a knife, money. I cursed myself for being impulsive. I wished I could tell the time by the sun. I looked back. I couldn't see the bay any more, nothing but bracken and peat, and grey, brown, green hills. Supposing we are walking in a circle, I thought. Supposing we find ourselves back by the house with Mr Carli waiting for us. Supposing we fail.

It was then that I heard an aeroplane droning overhead. Mr Carli, my mind screamed. Mr

Carli and George, armed to the teeth. I saw a hollow, dived for it, dragging a reluctant Phantom, who had decided I was mad and was not co-operating any more. There were rowan-trees in the hollow, rocks, even a sort of cave with bracken growing everywhere. I pulled Phantom towards the cave and cursed him when he would not move.

I stood beneath the rocks and waited. I wondered if Mr Carli had binoculars. Could he take aerial photographs as they did in wars and enlarge them afterwards? My brain ran riot. I imagined Angus and Hans locked in a room, one of the Australian horses being shot. The headlines in the papers. A hoof sent to the Australians to prove that their horse was really dead; a piece of ear – wasn't that more likely? But the aeroplane had gone now. I pulled Phantom after me and started to climb again. Now I hated the hills, longed for home as one longs for water when one is thirsty, for the cool beech-woods so sombre and peaceful; for the dreaming trees, the tracks thick with rustling leaves in autumn, thicker than the thickest carpet; for the telephone and the motorists passing along the road, for the feeling that help was always near, that one was not alone.

We reached the summit of the hill, and there was still another hill. I sat down and looked at it while Phantom nudged my back and the flies swarmed around his head. When I am home I will never complain again, I thought. I shall be so happy, so relieved, it will be like a dream come true.

"But we've got to go on," I told Phantom. "There is no other way."

It is supposed to be eight miles, I thought, to the other side. But eight miles up and down these hills is like fifty on the flat. How will we ever make the other side? Phantom was dragging now. He had lost faith in me, was convinced we were lost. He was right of course. Horses usually are. They have a way of knowing when you are scared or lost. He looked at me with his dark eyes and refused to budge. 'I want to go back,' he said, as plainly as though he were speaking.

"Walk on," I shouted, and hit him with the reins, ignoring the hurt look in his eyes.

We came to a burn and drank. The sun had moved, even I could see that – I who had never taken an interest in such things before. We came to a waterfall, alone and unadmired, and then to the ruins of old cottages which suddenly gave me hope. Then our sheep path widened and became a track. Phantom pricked his ears and hope came back into his eyes. Now the smell was different and we could feel salt in the air. The sky was decorated by seagulls like birds on wallpaper. I did not dare to hope.

"There will be another hill, Phantom," I told him. "Another and another. Or we will be back by the house on the wrong side of the island."

There were butterflies in my stomach, while my mind prayed, God, make it all right. God, let Angus be safe.

I ran to the top of this hill, dragging Phantom behind me, and below lay the sea. It was different from the sea I had left, or so it seemed, and Tuath was there before us, with telephone lines and houses, safe and civilised. I then threw my arms round Phantom and cried, "We've nearly made it. Only a little further. Come on, hurry, please hurry." Then I was running, stumbling over hillock and rock while below us lay white sands, whiter than I had ever seen before.

There are moments you never forget. This was one of them. I still dream of those white sands and the seals we saw playing there. The sea was gentle, washing the sands with its foam like soap bubbles, its sound as gentle as a breeze blowing through trees. There was no fear, the seals did not run at our approach and the gulls, which were everywhere, ignored us. The landscape belonged to them. We were the intruders with our sweaty bodies and our worldly worries.

I patted Phantom, unbuckled his girth and took off his saddle. I put it carefully on a rock and said goodbye to it in my heart.

Putting my arms round Phantom's neck, I said, "We've still got to reach Tuath. We haven't finished yet."

He looked at the sea and blew through his nostrils. I wondered whether he had ever been in salt water before; if he understood – if he could swim. I thought of Angus and Hans.

Were they saving the horses? Or were they out of the fight? Was I the only one left in it?

"We have to swim, Phantom," I said. "You know how, because you know everything."

I kicked off my riding-boots, then took off my hat and placed them by the saddle. "Keep calm, Jean," I told myself. "You are going to be all right."

I vaulted on to his back and together we stared at the glimmering expanse of sea. Tuath looked peaceful, a dreamland with a church spire and people like dots on the sand. Already

I seemed a long way from the school, from the children struggling to get through their entrance exams, from the pottery teacher with his thick-lensed glasses and bald patch on his head, from Miss Pitcher who made me think of a dishcloth gone dry and stringy with age, and from Caroline whom I did not understand.

I could believe that George and Mr Carli were criminals, but what about the others? Surely not. I knew now that I was simply putting off the moment of going into the sea. My thoughts were useless, they would change nothing. The other people did not matter, guilty or innocent. It was reaching Tuath which mattered, and raising the alarm, nothing else.

Phantom hesitated too, he could not believe my request. He looked at the sea and snorted, tasted it and retreated, curling his lip. I turned him round, reasoned with him, then suddenly realised that time was running out, that the sun had moved again, that morning was long gone and evening soon to come. "Walk on," I shouted, drumming his sides with my heels.

I could feel him trembling underneath me; his whole body going tense, his eyes widening, his neck arching with surprise.

"Walk on," I shouted. "Where's your courage?" I could feel my own draining away.

He put one hoof gingerly in the sea as though he was testing it, then started to walk forward, his hoofs sinking into the sand. I patted his neck again, leaning forward, knowing that in a minute he would have to swim.

The sea reached his knees, his shoulders, my legs. It was cold, so cold it took my breath away. I felt his hoofs lose touch with the earth, his head came up, his nostrils extended; then we were swimming.

9

Phantom's silver mane was half buried amid the waves, his neat ears stood straight up, his nostrils snorted. In front of us lay tiny islands clad with seaweed, beyond lay Tuath. Gradually the sea seemed less cold. Seals, whiskered and brown-grey, looked at us in mild surprise, then dived. The dots on the sand grew nearer and became people, the church took on new lines; the houses in the distance now had windows and doors. I steered Phantom gently towards an island, hardly daring to move. We were nearly there when I heard the aeroplane again. Phantom was scrambling through seaweed as strong as rope. The island was little more than solid rock, but some boulders were as large as men. I threw myself off and cried "Quick, Phantom. Move!" I dragged him between two large rocks and waited – trembling.

Phantom was very quiet and I could hear the aeroplane circling above us. But what could they do? I wondered. Where could they land?

Or would they shoot us with tranquilliser darts as if we were wild animals? Anything seemed possible as we waited between the rocks, shaking with cold. I wondered again what Angus was doing, whether the ransomed horses were still alive. Whether we would be in time to save anything at all, while gradually the sound of the engines ebbed away.

I led Phantom down to the sea again, struggling through more seaweed with him, told him it was nearly over. My head was throbbing, my legs turned to jelly. I struggled on to his back again, stared across at the dots which had become children gathering shells, at the houses so neat and white with curtains in their windows, and then we were swimming once more.

Minutes later we had hit sand. I slid to the ground. People were staring at us and pointing. My clothes clung to me, my hair hung down my back.

"I need a telephone," I yelled, running, dragging Phantom after me, both of us stumbling through the waves. Phantom was marvellous. He followed me as though he was competing in a gymkhana, his hoofs sending up great spurts of spray. A fat woman pointed to a house. "There's a phone over there," she called.

"What's happened? Is someone drowned?" asked a man.

"There's been a shipwreck, hasn't there?"

cried a small boy, his eyes alight with excitement. I reached the road. An idiot in a van gave a wolf-whistle. The road felt hard under my feet. A man was delivering bread. It all seemed insanely normal, yet a few miles away lives were in danger, human as well as equine. I then reached the house with the telephone. It was a small white farmhouse. I tied Phantom to a dilapidated gate and hammered on the door. A young man opened it. He had brown eyes, and he asked, "And who are you? A mermaid?"

Inwardly I thought, Fool! while I cried, "I need a telephone, quickly please, it's terribly urgent."

"Has a ship gone down?" he asked.

"No, not yet."

A woman appeared, carrying a baby, and for a terrible moment everything seemed to be in slow motion while she asked, "What is it? Who is she? Holy mother, she's wringing wet."

"A telephone. I need a telephone," I cried.

The man pointed. "Over there. Help yourself," he said.

My hair dripped on to a small antique table as I dialled 999 and asked for the police. I was shaking with a mixture of fear and cold, my bare feet had left a wet path across the patterned carpet.

"I'm from the island of Uaine," I said, without looking round, surprised that they couldn't hear the thudding of my heart. Then I was through to the police, trying to explain, but my voice was panic-stricken, and I gabbled, longing for a grown-up to take over. I could hear a keyboard in the background and I thought, at least they are putting it down, while I said, "The kidnapped Australian horses are on Uaine. I've just come from there." Even to my ears it sounded impossible, though I knew it was true. But I went on talking about my brother and Hans, about Mr Carli and George, about the whole beastly set-up. And all the time I was seeing them shooting the horses, one by one.

"You must be quick," I gabbled.

The man at the other end was so calm he made me want to scream.

"We are investigating. We have a great many calls coming in about the horses. We are investigating each one, but you must realise it takes time," he said in a sane English voice.

"But there isn't any time," I cried. "There's none left."

I gave him my name, my home address, I mentioned my father. I tried to sound calm, but I couldn't. At last I put down the receiver and, holding my head in my hands, cried, "What am I going to do?"

Someone had put a towel round my shoulders while I talked. The woman handed me a mug of tea. Suddenly the room started to go round so I sat on the arm of a chair.

"They aren't here, are they?" I asked. "There isn't a plane landing? I swam all the way with Phantom, my horse. He's still all right, isn't he?" I rushed to the door and looked outside.

Phantom was standing looking half drowned, while one hind leg dripped blood on to the rough stones. There was no sign of George or

Mr Carli, and for a second the whole thing seemed like a dream. In a minute I will wake up and find myself in bed at Sparrow Cottage, I thought, with Dad picking up the letters off the hall mat. I shall eat breakfast in the kitchen and go outside and school Phantom . . . But, of course, it was true. And, however awful, I had to do something. Then I remembered about the number Dad gave us when he went away – I had left it behind in my hat. I should have carried it in my mouth, I thought. What a fool I am!

"Calm down. What's your name? You're in a terrible state," said the woman, as though I was excited about nothing.

But now I had thought of Dominic. I picked up the receiver and dialled his number.

"Whoever you are, you have plenty of cheek," the woman said.

"I'm sorry," I cried, praying that Dominic would answer, seeing his farm bathed in sunlight with the cows leaving the milking parlour slowly, like old women.

"It's Jean," I shouted. "Please can I speak to Dominic?"

"Speaking. What is it? Where are you?"

I'd forgotten how calm he always sounded, as though nothing would ever drive him to hysteria, while behind me I heard the woman say, "I think she needs a doctor. I do really . . ."

"Listen!" I shouted. "It's very important." By this time I could hardly believe what I was about to say myself. I couldn't believe that I was even speaking to Dominic. I felt as though it was someone else standing in a strange house talking about kidnapped horses held to ransom. "It's true, it really is, Dominic, please believe me," I finished. "It's happening now. Angus is on the island with the crooks; they'll kill him and the horses any minute."

"I know about the horses. Okay. I have your address. You gave it to me. Yes, I will convince the police; I'll take Dad with me and you know how convincing he is," said Dominic, and for a second I saw Mr Barnes in his braces, with his cap on the back of his head; the sort of man who won't budge until he has had his say.

Silently I thanked God for all the Mr Barneses in this world. "Please hurry," I said.

"But are you all right?" he asked, making me sound more important than the horses or the danger to Angus and Hans.

"Yes, but Angus isn't."

"Not to worry. I'll get to work straight away. Goodbye." He rang off as the room started to spin round again.

"Are you sure you know what you're talking about?" asked the woman. Her voice came to me through a haze of exhaustion as I saw that she had red-brown hair and a long nose. "All that talk about kidnapped horses; it sounds the most utter rubbish to me," she continued. "And what on earth were you doing in the sea? Have you run away from some institution?"

"Only from the island of Uaine. Perhaps you know it, perhaps you know Mr Carli, perhaps you even like him." My voice was slurred; I knew I sounded drunk, but I could do nothing about it.

"She's completely round the bend. We must do something, Chris," the woman said.

"Can't you lend her a pair of jeans and some shoes?" asked Chris, taking the baby from her.

The tea had grown cold. They gave me jeans which were too big, a man's sweater and canvas shoes. I muttered my thanks, dressed and went outside to see Phantom. He was still bleeding.

"Have you got a bandage? Anything. Torn up sheet will do," I asked.

I felt as though it was someone else talking. I wasn't really there any more. I was a bystander watching someone called Jean Simpson performing. I was afraid of passing out. I found a pebble, wrapped it in the handkerchief Chris gave me, put it on Phantom's wound and held it there. I held on to his other leg or I would have fainted, for the yard kept going round just as the room had done. "Is it bad?" asked Chris.

"Middling," answered Jean Simpson, while I watched.

The woman brought a gauze bandage. "Does he need food?" she asked. "A bed?"

"Yes, he does," replied Jean Simpson.

"Turn him out in the field then."

"Thank you," answered Jean politely.

The bleeding was stopping and evening had come, all red and gold. I bandaged Phantom's leg with the pebble still in place over the wound. He nuzzled my hair as I stood up and waited for everything to stop going round, before I led him to the small field nearby. There were wild irises by its gate and pinks growing amid rocks strewn at random everywhere, as though someone had just stopped playing with them.

"You had better come and sit down," suggested Chris. "You don't look too good."

They pushed me into a chair and gave me cracker biscuits and a glass of milk. They asked my name and what my father did, and why I had gone to Uaine. I tried to tell them, but all the time my story seemed more and more improbable until I hardly believed in it myself.

"But you can't have swum all that way," the woman said.

"I didn't, Phantom did." Nothing seemed to taste any more; and the biscuits turned to sand in my mouth.

I said, "I'm sorry about being a nuisance, and I'm sorry about the telephone calls. I have masses of money on Uaine. I'll pay you back, and if it's disappeared, and things do disappear there, my father will settle up with you. He's in the Middle East, soothing things down."

They looked at me in amazement. I might have come from outer space the way they looked. Then they looked at each other and the woman muttered, "Yes, I think so," and went to the telephone.

"It is true. It really is. Don't you listen to the news?" I asked. But they weren't attending any more. They had made up their minds – I was insane. I had better leave, I thought. But now my legs which had never let me down before refused to move, and my eyes wouldn't stay open. I must have fallen asleep, for the next thing I knew was a policeman shaking me by the shoulder. He wore a uniform; his shoes and buttons glistened.

"Where am I?" I cried, and then, "Thank goodness you're here."

10

The policeman had a broad Scottish accent, so broad that I could hardly understand him. He said he wanted to know the lie of the land. He produced a map, while I kept saying, "Please hurry."

"We don't want anyone killed," he said, or words to that effect.

I drew a picture of everything, while the man and the woman stood behind me looking disagreeable because I was not mad after all.

Gradually more police came, and they talked about boats and asked me about the landing-strip. I said, "There could be two smashed-up planes on it," and imagined Hans and Angus destroying them, if they were still there, if they were still alive. They talked about a contingent from the mainland, and I said, "Please can I come too? I may be able to help."

I went on and on until one of them relented, and the woman gave me a coat because a policeman told her to, and I rushed out to look

at Phantom. The bandage was still on and the bleeding had stopped.

Ten minutes later I was on a boat speeding back to Uaine. They told me to stay on the boat, to keep out of mischief.

They did not want any more trouble, they said, and laughed and talked about mermaids. The island looked beautiful in the gathering darkness, lit by the dying rays of the sun. Too beautiful for man to spoil. It should be left to the animals, I thought, to the sheep, goats and deer. The coastline loomed rocky and wild and then we were landing. "Keep back, and keep out of mischief," the first policeman said. "We'll call you if we need you."

"What do you mean?" I asked.

"Stay in the boat, lass, that's what we mean," he said.

"You'll need me to sort out the horses," I muttered. "And I know everyone. You can't manage without me."

"You'd be surprised," said a cheeky one, over his shoulder.

I was scared again, scared for Angus, scared I would find him dead somewhere, or worse still, not find him at all.

Then lights started to move around the square, the policemen's lights. Mr Carli will have fled to the mainland by now, I thought. He will have jumped in a boat with Maria and George. By tomorrow they'll be miles away, basking in the sun on some foreign beach, or sipping drinks by a swimming-pool. They will never catch them. But what about Angus and the others? Were they still on the island or gone too?

Then I saw that the house was burning. Flames were turning the sky orange, lighting up the rhododendrons where Mr Carli had walked in the mornings, and the lawn where the guests had played rounders. Then I was running towards the house, crying, "Angus is inside. Angus and Hans. We've got to get them out."

A policeman caught me. Timbers were falling, everything was caving in. "Do you want to get killed, love? Is that what you're wanting?" he asked.

I knew there was no hope, that anyone inside would have perished. "There could be a bomb inside," said the policeman. "There's nothing anyone can do."

He let me loose and I ran to the square, but it was empty too – the gates open, the doors gaping wide, the horses gone. I'm too late! I thought. We were all too late. If only I had swum faster or found help quicker. If only the police hadn't dithered. If only I had made them understand the situation. I wished that I had stayed on Uaine and perished with Angus. I did not want to go on living, not even with Phantom. I sat on a rock and tried to stem the tears pouring down my face, while a policeman talked into a radio, announcing that the square was empty, asking for instructions.

Then I heard footsteps on the path and Angus's voice behind me, calling, "Sorry we couldn't save the house. We couldn't save everything. Has anyone seen my sister? She tried to swim the sea on a palomino called Phantom," and he was half laughing, half crying.

His face was blackened and smiling, and Hans was behind him.

"It's nice to see you at last," said my brother, with laughter in his eyes. I knew at once that we were in time, that I had not failed.

Hans took my hand and kissed it. His eyes glistened with tears. "And your little golden horse, did he swim?" he asked, trying to laugh.

I nodded, unable to speak and overcome by Hans's emotion.

"Yes, he was marvellous," I said at last, "but he's very tired."

"Pity about the house," said Angus. "It must have been full of evidence."

"And the horses?" I asked.

"All right. Caroline let them loose. Her love of horses overcame her love for her father, I suppose."

"And the children? They're not still in the house?" I cried.

Angus shook his head "Of course not," he said. "I think I had better tell you everything," he said. "But first, have you got anything to eat?"

"No, not a thing, sorry," I said.

"Never mind. Hans, you will keep me on the right track, won't you?" asked Angus. "After you had gone, there was turmoil. Caroline appeared at lunch to announce that you had gone off on Phantom and were lost. Mr Carli raved and ranted and then ran out of the house and up to the airstrip, and a minute later we heard his plane starting up. Everyone else seemed to believe that you were really lost, or pretended to be . . . Hans and I could not look at each other for fear of giving the game away. No one ate much after that. In half an hour Mr Carli was back. He took Caroline into his office, while Mr Smith, you know, the pottery chap, organised games on the front lawn to keep us out of mischief. Then Mr Carli disappeared again in his plane, and Hans and I slipped down to the square where we found Caroline preparing for the slaughter of the horses."

"What do you mean?" I asked.

"She had a humane killer and a twitch," answered Angus. "Hans twisted her arm, didn't you, Hans? Then she started weeping. We collected all her poisons out of the tack room, opened the yard gates and took the horses down to the field by the house – and it wasn't easy I can tell you."

"Then we threw everything into a binbag and dumped it in the sea, poisons, twitch, humane killer, everything," said Hans.

"Then we heard Mr Carli coming back," continued Angus. "We hid until he was in the house and then slipped up to the airstrip. Hans understands planes. He got inside with a knife and screwdriver. Then we found some tools in the shed near the airstrip and hammered holes in the fuel tanks for good measure. Then we made for the boats."

"What about Jacques?" I asked.

"He was in the boathouse with Janet."

"With Janet?"

"Yes, they are lovers," said my brother, without batting an eyelid. "That's why he is here. He met Janet when he came to Scotland on holiday last year. Hans found that out this afternoon, too late to be of any use."

"So we left them in the boathouse and bashed holes in the boats. It was terrific fun until Mr Carli heard the noise," continued Angus, pausing for breath.

"What then? I'm riveted," I cried, and it was true. All my tiredness had gone. I was so relieved that Angus and Hans were safe that I felt uplifted to a new height of happiness.

"We ran away, didn't we, Hans? But before we went, I shouted, 'You're finished, Mr Carli. You can't get off the island, and Jean is fetching help. You've lost.'"

"He turned mad. He hurled rocks at us, did he not, Angus?" asked Hans. "Yes, like an angry little boy. I stayed and taunted him, while Angus slipped up to the house," he continued. "I enjoyed it."

"I found the children with Miss Pitcher. I said, 'Mr Carli has gone mad, get the children out,' and I must say she was marvellous. She blew her whistle and called out, 'Line up two and two, quick march,' and counted them. We marched them down to the maths room."

"And everybody else?" I asked.

"All safe. Jane took a bit of persuading. Poor Mr Matheson wouldn't join us for ages, not till he saw Mr Carli coming up to the house, bellowing like a madman . . ."

"And Mr Smith?"

"He was a hero. When Mr Carli started setting fire to the place with George, he tried to stop them, and got his spectacles smashed for his pains and came out like something blind," said Angus.

"And Maria?"

"She's gone with the others."

"So who are the police hunting now?"

"Mr Carli, Caroline, George and Maria."

"So Caroline was guilty too?" I asked.

"That's right. But you look awful, Jean. Whoever gave you those terrible clothes?"

"Shut up. She saved our lives. Your queen should give her a medal," said Hans.

I looked at the house. The flames were subsiding, the turrets were still there, blackened, with the glass gone from their windows.

"I suppose all our things have gone up in flames?" I said.

"Most of them, but I've got our money and Grandpa's binoculars," replied Angus.

"You must be happy," I told Hans.

"Not yet, not until Carli's caught. He may still swim to Tuath," said Hans.

A helicopter was coming in to land.

"They are bringing more men and the dogs," a policeman said.

"Hooray, can we follow the hunt on horses?" asked Angus.

"If you can catch them."

We walked up to the maths room. A policeman was questioning everyone in turn. It still smelled like a classroom in spite of the smoke wafting past the windows.

The policeman looked at us and said, "We

will need to talk to you in a minute."

Jane was red in the face. "I don't know where Daddy is. He doesn't want me, anyway," she gasped.

Janet was feeding her baby. She smiled at us while Jacques sat holding her hand.

"What about your mother, dear?" asked the policeman.

"She doesn't want me either," said Jane.

"Tell us how it really happened; how it all began," requested Angus.

"We don't really know. We think the horse box driver was involved. He's in custody. Someone must have given details of the horses' movements," replied an unmistakably English policeman.

"You mean the Australian driver?" Angus asked.

"They didn't have an Australian driver. They used a hired horse box."

"Were they going to a show?" I asked.

"I believe so."

"And the box was stopped and the driver chucked out, but unhurt?" asked Angus.

The policeman nodded. "And then the box was abandoned?" I suggested.

"And the ransom note?" asked Angus.

"They telephoned."

"It will be in all the papers," said the policeman. "Buy them on Sunday."

"When is that?"

"The day after tomorrow."

"You know George, don't you?" I asked next. "He's been in prison, hasn't he?"

"They reckon so, but I can't talk any more, I have to go," the policeman said.

"What about Mr Carli? Do you know him?" I cried.

"You'll have to ask Interpol that," he said.

"So Hans is right," I cried. "He is an international crook. We must tell Hans. Where is he?"

"Mr Carli is wanted in Germany for intimidation, in Denmark for drug smuggling, and in France for blackmail," said the policeman.

"One more thing," cried Angus. "Were the Australians willing to pay up?"

"No, never. You see if they had it would have set a precedent. Kidnapping horses might become big business; besides, the owners haven't that sort of money."

We followed him outside. "Let's see the horses," suggested Angus. "Hans is looking for Mr Carli."

"Who has lots of other names," I said.

"Yes, of course," agreed Angus.

We walked along the path through the rhododendrons. I remembered Mr Carli walking through them swinging his arms. It all seemed to have happened a long time ago. In a way I had loved my bedroom with its sumptuous bed and glorious view. Now it was gone too.

"Are you tired?" asked Angus.

"Yes, but happy too. He's nice, isn't he?" I asked.

"Who?"

"Hans."

"And efficient. He knew just what to do with the planes. He's a genius in his way. He could manage the horses too," said Angus. We had reached the field where I had schooled so often. The jumps lay scattered. The horses stood in a huddle. They threw up their heads at our approach. They were no longer tranquillised dummies, but real and afraid.

"They're lovely," I said.

"They would have been killed. We were only just in time. If Mr Carli had not pursued you and Phantom, we might have been too late."

"That's life," I said. "Everything hangs in the balance, full of 'if onlys' and 'too lates'."

I climbed the gate, talking to the horses. "We're friends," I said. "No more injections, you're going home."

Milestone started to pace round the field like a mustang, and soon all the horses were pounding round, their tails high.

"We'll never catch them. Let's go back," said Angus.

"I wonder what the others are called. I hope

they win next year's Olympics," I said.

"So do I," agreed Angus.

"Is it night or morning?" I asked, following Angus back along the path through the rhododendrons.

"I'm not sure. It was night, but the burning house lit up everything; now I think it's almost morning," Angus told me. "Another day. Think on that."

"Yes, there was a moon. I remember seeing it," I answered. Then I started to worry about Phantom, about his cut, the pebble and the possibility of his bleeding to death.

We had reached the square again. "You are just in time," a policeman said. "They are being brought in."

We stood and waited. The sky was light with rose and pink spreading from the east. Everybody looked tired, for it had been a long night. They were coming down from the hills protesting loudly.

"You'll be sorry for this," shouted Mr Carli. "Very sorry. I know a lot of people in high places."

"They're different horses. They have nothing to do with Australia," said Maria, who had a scarf over her head.

Caroline said nothing. She looked beaten, and inwardly I wept for her. She looked away when I tried to catch her eye, and I guessed that

everything had begun a long time ago, that she had never meant to be involved, that somehow she had been caught like a fly in a spider's web, her father's web. She had never got free.

George was very red in the face. From the way the police spoke to him, we knew they had met him before.

"It's sad, and I never expected it to be sad," I said.

"Not for me; for me it is glorious," answered Hans. "It is justice at last."

"You will be sorry for this, Jean," said Mr Carli, looking straight at me. "You need help. Horse-mad girls always do."

"I wish you had drowned, you and your damned horse," said George.

"And you are wrong about the horses – quite wrong," shouted Mr Carli.

"They will be identified soon enough, Mr Carli," said a policeman, looking at his watch. "It has been a long night and I advise you to come quietly."

"They are not the ones held to ransom. They are a different lot altogether. You should never listen to Caroline, she is not reliable; she isn't stable, she never has been," Mr Carli shouted wildly.

I thought of them being taken to court. Would they have blankets over their heads?

"Maria is his girlfriend. I had suspected that

all along," said Angus, "so everything falls into place, doesn't it? Everyone else, except for George and the mysterious woman who came in the night with the horses, is in the clear. And I'm glad."

Jon was coming towards us. He held out his hand.

"Well done," he said. "You have won."

But it did not feel like winning, perhaps because we had never wanted to enter. We had come to enjoy ourselves, not to compete.

The children were out of the classroom now, running, screaming and leaping towards the sea, like a pack of hounds just let out of kennel.

"Steady, moderation in all things," called Miss Pitcher, but they were out of control, pushing and fighting each other on the sand.

Mr Smith said sadly, "I should have known. I should never have left it to you kids. I had no idea the horses were even here. Why didn't you come to me for help?"

"Because we didn't trust you," answered Angus. "We didn't trust anyone once I realised that Maria was collaborating with Mr Carli. It was such a shock."

I remembered how Angus had admired her right from the start. Then Mr Smith asked, "Is that Jean? I can't see anything without my spectacles, but I want to shake your hand. I never thought you had it in you to undertake such a swim. I misjudged you completely. You see, I have never liked horsy girls."

His handshake was firm and long-lasting. I took my hand away at last. Our task was finished. I wanted to be with Phantom again, nothing else at that moment, only that. But the policeman who seemed to be in charge told us that the Australian trainer would be arriving at any minute to look at the horses. "And you're booked into the Flora Macdonald Hotel on Tuath for the night, and then you can go home," he told us.

Angus said, "We must speak to our parents first." The policeman said that it could be arranged and that nothing was too much trouble for such a brave lad and lassie.

I said, "What about Hans?"

"I'm looking after myself," replied Hans. "I'm all right."

"They haven't wasted much time, have they?" I asked.

"Who?"

"The police."

"Not now, not once they were here. But they were a long time arriving. It was awful waiting for them, you'll never know how awful," said Angus.

A boat was approaching the jetty.

"This is it. This is the moment of truth," announced Angus.

I went pale. I know my hands started to shake and I thought, Supposing it was all for nothing? Supposing we'd made a mistake? How will we ever live it down? Supposing the grey wasn't Milestone after all?

Hans put an arm around me. "Do not worry, everything is going to be all right, Jean," he said. "I tell you, I know."

Two young Australians leaped from the boat. "Okay, where are they then?" they cried.

"Follow me," said Angus, looking rather wan. "We can't catch them, but perhaps you can."

Behind us, the children were lining up to get on the boat which had brought the Australians. I could hear Miss Pitcher's shrill voice calling, "Two by two. Not that way, Rachel dear. Matthew, come here at once . . ."

11

The Australians were lean and fit, and they walked too fast for us. Running to keep up, I knew how tired we were, even Hans, who until now had seemed to possess the strength of ten men. We were like flat batteries which needed recharging.

"My, what a place!" exclaimed one of the Australians. "My forebears came from Scotland. They left at the time of the Clearances. Think of that!"

"There they are. In the field over there," said Angus pointing, his voice trembling a little.

"Are they your horses?" I asked. I looked at Angus and knew that we both felt like screaming with suspense.

The Australians didn't reply. They simply called the horses, using pet names. Angus smiled, a smile which stretched from ear to ear.

"Well? Yes or no?" he cried.

"Yeah. They are ours all right."

I sank into the heather. For a moment I had

no strength left. Angus gave them the headcollars we had carried. The horses were pacing round the field, playing games, snorting and prancing, looking beautiful beyond words in the early morning light.

"We were right then. Oh, I'm so tired," said Angus, sinking down beside me.

The Australians were pulling their horses' ears, running their hands down their legs, overcome with emotion at finding them. I knew

how they felt. How they must have suffered, wondering whether they would ever see them again.

"My legs ache and I want to see Phantom. He has a bad wound and if the bandage comes off, the flies will be eating it – and I want to go home," I said.

"Home?" exclaimed Angus. "It seems years since we were there."

"A whole century," I said.

We walked back towards the square, past the burnt house still smouldering in places, with our belongings turned to ash inside.

"We've lost almost everything. It's lucky I thought of the money, otherwise we would be penniless. I hope my radio and camera were insured," said Angus, stopping to look.

"It's sad, but it's not the end, worse things could have happened," I said. "Phantom could be dead."

I thought of my hat, boots and saddle, on the other side of Uaine. It seemed years since I had left them there. I remembered the seals and how beautiful it had been and how I was afraid, and I felt so grateful to be alive, so grateful that everything looked twice as beautiful as it had before.

"People are not exactly thanking us, are they?" I asked. "I mean, we tipped off the police, told them everything, nearly died, and no one's even said thank you to us yet."

"I know. You were pretty efficient. How did you do it?" asked Angus.

"I think it was Dominic," I answered. "The local police weren't really interested, so I rang him. He must have convinced them that I wasn't just one more nutcase."

When we reached the jetty again, Mr Carli and all the other residents had gone. Only Hans was left, sitting on a rock, swinging his long legs, while he waited for us.

"I need clothes," he said. "Look at me. I look filthy, yes?"

"Where will you go next?" I asked.

"Home to Germany, to my mother. She will be anxious, you know how mothers are. But I will be back, never fear."

I knew he would be all right. He is the sort of person who can manage life, like Dominic, but with more drive and ambition.

"You can stay with us," offered Angus.

"Thank you. That will be very nice. And you can stay with me. Jean can ride one of our great dressage horses. Germany produces many dressage horses, all of the finest calibre."

"What about clean clothes?" I asked.

Hans patted his pockets. "I have money. It is no problem. I will wash and then go to the shops," he said.

"Perhaps we can visit you next summer," said

Angus. "Plus Phantom, of course, otherwise we can't, can we, Jean?"

"Shut up," I said.

Hans kissed us both before he left, sitting up very straight on a police boat, surrounded by policemen, waving and waving.

"Do you think we'll ever see him again?" I asked.

"Yes, of course. I have his address. We can go there next time Dad disappears to Asia, China, or wherever he's sent to next, and you can study dressage and I will learn German, and we'll be very sensible. No hassle, no problem, easy as pie."

A policeman was signalling to us, explaining that we were wanted for questioning. He was very apologetic and promised to make it as quick as possible. "Because you look awful weary," he said.

Later on we too left. The sun had dipped behind the hills. The Highland ponies watched from a field, everything was suddenly green and empty.

"Don't cry," said Angus. "I can see your eyes are watering."

"Shut up. Why should I cry?" I asked.

The policemen with us were tired and silent. The sea was calm and gentle, the sky a cloud-scattered blue. It's the end of a dream, I thought. A dream which went wrong.

Phantom was standing by the gate with the irises round it. He whinnied when he saw me. He looked tired and his coat smelled of the sea. But the bandage was still on and there was no blood seeping through.

The Flora Macdonald Hotel was full of middle-aged parents with children, single women and ardent bird-watchers. My room had a pink bedspread on the bed and flowered wallpaper. It was old-fashioned with a fireplace and a huge walnut wardrobe. I sat on my bed and almost at once there was a knock at the door and a slim girl appeared.

"I've come to lend you some clothes," she said. "I'm a student from England working here, and you've been asked out to lunch by the manager of the Australian team. Mrs Macdonald thought you might need help."

"Are you sure?" I asked. She had hazel eyes and freckles round her nose. She told me she was called Mel.

"I really think you deserve a medal," she told me. "I do really. How ever did you swim all that way?"

I realised that the story must be all over the island now and wherever I went there would be someone staring at me. Because I was basically shy it wasn't a nice feeling.

"It wasn't me, it was Phantom. He has

tremendous courage. I couldn't have done it without him," I said.

"If you had waited a bit, it would have been low tide," she said, holding out a dress.

"I couldn't wait."

She sat on my bed while I tried on her dresses. She told me that she once owned a pony called Messenger.

I put on a plain dress, sandals and a dark blue blazer. They fitted me perfectly.

"You look marvellous," she said. "They suit you better than they do me." I knew she was the sort of person who always belittles herself.

"Rubbish," I said, looking at myself in the mirror, seeing a red face, bleary eyes, nut-brown hair stiff with salt.

"And I'm proud to have met you," said Mel, getting off my bed and scooping up the unwanted dresses.

"Don't be silly, I'm nothing special. Anyone else would have done the same."

"Oh, yeah, sure. Just leave the clothes on the chair when you've finished with them."

"Thank you a million times," I said.

"The Australians will meet you in the hall in twenty minutes. Good luck," she said, shutting the door after her.

I thought, She's so nice and so generous, she is hardly real. I felt quite different dressed in her clothes.

The Australians, who were called Bill and
Jason, treated us to an enormous meal. I was
too tired to take much in, but I remembered
they offered us reward money and a trip to
Australia with Phantom, and tickets for next
year's Olympics. They wanted to know every
detail of what had happened several times over,
paid us lavish compliments, and plied us with
red wine. There were candles on the tables and
red paper napkins, and the sound of the sea
outside. I remember asking them to look after
the Highland ponies and I told them about the
sheep which needed shearing, and because they

were from Australia they understood. Some time later when we had reached the coffee stage, our parents rang. I staggered to the telephone and asked, "How did you know we were here?"

Mum said, "We're not imbeciles. As soon as we heard that the ransomed horses had been hidden on a Scottish island we knew you would be in the thick of it. We telephoned the police, we've been in touch for the last eight hours. Are you all right?"

"Yes, just a bit peculiar," I answered, "and a bit too full of food."

"We're returning home. We've finished here," she said, before Angus snatched the receiver from me to shout:

"You don't have to, we are perfectly all right. We are not ten-year-olds."

Then Dad came on the line. "Don't talk to journalists. A national newspaper wants to buy your story. There's also going to be a television interview," he said.

"But we're too tired," replied Angus. "We want to forget the whole thing. It wasn't fun. It was awful."

"You can't forget it. They won't let you," replied Dad. "The only thing is to organise everything in a civilised way, otherwise they'll be fighting over you. We'll talk about it when we meet. In the meantime, keep your mouths shut. How's Phantom?"

"In no fit state to talk," answered Angus, beginning to laugh.

Before going to bed, I paid Phantom one last visit. He was lying down, his pale hoofs tucked under him. I sat with him and told him that he was better than all the humans in the entire world, and the bravest horse that had ever lived. But I don't think he understood. So I said, "We're going home. Back to Sparrow Cottage," and he put his head on my shoulder and shut his eyes.

Later, walking back to the hotel, I wondered how we would ever make it. Uaine was dim on the horizon, but Sparrow Cottage seemed a million miles away. I undressed and folded up Mel's clothes and saw that clean jeans had been provided, a blue shirt and a sweater – I suddenly felt overwhelmed by so much kindness. When I lay down, my bed felt like heaven. In seconds the world floated away into a wonderful dreamless sleep.

I awakened to hear a strange voice saying, "We have a visitor for you, Jean. He's waiting downstairs in the hall. He's come a wee way."

Who now? I thought. "If it's the Press, tell them to go away," I said, without opening my eyes.

"He's no pressman," continued the voice, "and he wants to see you awful bad."

It must be Hans, I thought.

"All right, I'm on my way, and thank you," I said. I looked at the clothes provided – the others had disappeared. I dragged a comb through my hair and thought how terrible I looked, like someone just washed-up on the beach. I put on the clothes and walked down-stairs slowly, holding on to the banister because I seemed to have seized up in the night – all my joints creaked and my legs felt like lead. I found Dominic. He was standing in the hall, holding his cap in his hand, suntanned and solid.

"I've come to take you home," he said, sounding like a father fetching his daughter from a dance.

"How did you get here?" I cried.

"Aren't you pleased?"

"Of course I am. I'm just amazed to see you. It's like a miracle." He looked civilised and clean, which made me twice as conscious of my own tatty appearance.

"But what about Phantom? I have to get him home too," I cried.

Sighing, he said, "That's the whole point, Jean, I've brought the trailer. It's outside. I drove the whole night and caught the first ferry. It was full of pressmen coming to interview you, so you had better hurry. You're both famous, Jean, didn't you know?"

"And you are so marvellous, Dominic, we'll

never be able to thank you enough," I cried. "Where are the pressmen now?"

"Having breakfast in the posh hotel."

"What's the time?"

"Just gone seven."

"I'll wake Angus," I said, and twenty minutes later we were loading Phantom.

"How did you know we were here, Dominic?" asked Angus. "It's fantastic to see you."

"Everyone knows," he said.

"But it's only twenty-five past seven," exclaimed Angus, consulting his watch.

"Exactly. Walk on, Phantom, steady. He looks in a mess. What has he done to his leg? Did you really swim with him, Jean?" asked Dominic.

"Yes, and it was terrifying." But already the ordeal was fading, the sharp edges were growing blunt. I could no longer feel the seaweed clinging to our legs like rope, nor recall the fear I had felt as I rode him into the sea.

"I owe lots of people money, and what about the clothes I borrowed?" I asked.

"I sorted that out when I asked about the bill, which we are not allowed to pay. The clothes you borrowed are being washed and they will be returned clean to their owners, Mr and Mrs Jones. The ones you have on, you're to post back to Melanie Heelas at the hotel. Your jodhpurs are a write-off. Okay?"

"Marvellous, except for the jodhs," I said. Then I looked at my brother and saw that he was clean, fresher even than Dominic. "You've washed?" I gasped.

"Just a shower or two. You were too tired to notice yesterday. You looked like a hedgehog; your eyes had disappeared into your prickles. I've never seen you look like that before. You went to bed at seven, did you know?"

"I owe money for telephone calls," I said. "And I don't care when I went to bed."

Angus handed me a ten-pound note. "Stick it under their door."

"It's too much," I said.

"It doesn't matter."

So Dominic gave me a pen and paper and I wrote: *This is for everything. Many thanks, Jean Simpson,* and pushed it and the tenner under the door of the little farmhouse. Inside the baby was crying. I shut the gate where the irises grew. Phantom was loaded. The ramp was up, it was time to go.

"It will be eight hours hard driving. I'll have to stop for a kip halfway," said Dominic, starting the Land Rover's engine.

"We must avoid the pressmen," murmured Angus.

The island was coming to life as we boarded the eight o'clock ferry. Small children stood gazing at the sand as though it were paradise.

Housewifely women in pinnies shook mats, a few sleepy shopkeepers were pushing up their shutters. Cows stood by a gate, and the sun was already shining above the hills.

"Heaven and hell!" exclaimed Angus, as we left the pier.

"I never thought I would see Scotland," said Dominic, as though he had travelled miles to another world. "By the way, Killarney won the hunter class."

"Congratulations," said Angus.

I thought about my hat and my boots, lonely on an empty shore. Perhaps birds would nest in my hat. Perhaps years hence people would see them and ponder. Angus said my saddle did not matter.

"The national newspaper will be paying us a fortune," he told me. "So not to worry. You can have the best saddle made to measure with forward-cut flaps and a spring tree – the lot. And I shall be able to have a motor-bike."

Tuath was fading as the mainland grew near. I looked at the sea, but I didn't see it. Instead I saw Angus and me going to the Olympics as honoured guests; then crossing the outback on Phantom, and suddenly anything was possible, anything in the whole world.

Dominic looked at me and smiled and I knew that we were safe now because he would never let us down.

"I shall write to Caroline in prison," I said. "And to someone about the Highland ponies and sheep left on Uaine." But already the last few weeks were beginning to seem like a dream.

We were approaching Teanga harbour. There was a long line of cars on the jetty and cranes reaching into the sky. We've come back alive, I thought, clambering down the metal steps to the hold below. Phantom was standing calmly in the trailer munching the hay Dominic had brought. I am sure he knew we were going home.

There's not much else to tell. The journey was long and uneventful. Dominic needed to sleep the minute we had crossed the border into England. We stopped at a motorway service station and left him sleeping while we had coffee and bought a newspaper which had a terrible photograph of us taken years ago on the front page.

"Wherever did they get it?" moaned Angus. "It's so awful!"

"It must be a school one. Look, I've still got baby teeth, you're wearing a tie and your hair is all smooth and shining," I cried.

"Do we still look like that?"

"No. We're much scruffier now," I said.

There was one of Phantom in another paper. He had a rosette pinned to his bridle and I was simpering at nothing through the plaits in his mane. There was a caption underneath which

read: THEY SWAM TO GET HELP. Another newspaper announced that our whole exclusive story would be in their Sunday edition.

"We'll never escape now," moaned Angus. "We'll be labelled for life."

"If we have to go to court, I shall say nice things about Caroline, and I shall praise Hans to the skies, and we mustn't forget Janet," I said.

"I don't think we should be horrid about Maria either. I think she was the victim of circumstances and under Mr Carli's influence. He had a powerful personality, didn't he?" asked Angus, loyal to the last.

"He's not dead yet," I said.

"I think I'm going to train Phantom for horse trials. His dressage is super now and if I'm going to Germany with him, it will get even better. Caroline was a fantastic instructor," I said. "She taught me masses and I wrote it all down on file paper so that I could remember it for ever and ever."

"Where is it now?" asked Angus, laughing.

"Burned to ashes, I suppose," I replied.

"But I still have this," said Angus, holding out a little bowl. "It will be my souvenir."

"What is it?" I asked. "It looks a bit bent."

"Shut up. There's no need to be jealous. I made it in pottery class, and I shall keep it for ever," he said.

"I'm not jealous," I answered, "because I'm going to aim for the Badminton Horse Trials and we must go to Australia. We can't miss a chance like that."

"Yes," agreed Angus, "and I suppose Phantom has to come with us, but this time we'll keep out of trouble."

"Yes. We'll keep our ears and eyes firmly shut," I agreed, laughing, but I knew that we wouldn't, because we were simply not made that way.